I0739429

A Harmony Falls Novel
Book 3

Marrying the Wrong Man

ELLEY ARDEN

author of *Battling the Best Man* and
Crashing the Congressman's Wedding

CRIMSON
ROMANCE

F+W Media, Inc.

Copyright © 2014 by Elley Arden.
All rights reserved.
This book, or parts thereof, may not be reproduced in any form without permission from the publisher; exceptions are made for brief excerpts used in published reviews.

Published by
Crimson Romance
an imprint of F+W Media, Inc.
10151 Carver Road, Suite 200
Blue Ash, OH 45242. U.S.A.
www.crimsonromance.com

ISBN 10: 1-4405-7962-8
ISBN 13: 978-1-4405-7962-2
eISBN 10: 1-4405-7963-6
eISBN 13: 978-1-4405-7963-9

This is a work of fiction. Names, characters, corporations, institutions, organizations, events, or locales in this novel are either the product of the author's imagination or, if real, used fictitiously. The resemblance of any character to actual persons (living or dead) is entirely coincidental.

Cover art © iStockphoto.com/alvarez and iStockphoto.com/poiremolle

To Ange, Cyndi, Jackie, Sue, and Tammy. Good girlfriends are hard to find. I'm so glad I found you. Thank you for cheering me on.
XOXO

Acknowledgments

This book proves the sheer power of readers. After the first Harmony Falls book, *Crashing the Congressman's Wedding*, so many of you wrote about your love for Charlie and your hopes that he would get his own book, that I couldn't ignore you. I hope I've done him justice.

Thank you for reading and taking the time to share with me how the characters and stories touch your lives. You touch mine.

Chapter One

"There must be a mistake," Morgan Parrish said, as she blinked at the dull quarter in the palm of her hand.

"No mistake," the perky credit union teller replied. "Up until five seconds ago, the account balance was twenty-five cents."

Morgan's stomach flipped, causing a tidal wave of panic to obliterate rational thought. "That can't be. Check again." She leaned so far over the counter that the teller backed away. "Something is wrong with your screen. You're missing zeros. Lots of zeros. This account was established the day I was born. I've never made a single withdrawal in thirty-two years!"

"But the joint account owner, Kathleen Parrish, has." The young woman, who Morgan had picked expressly because she didn't recognize her, studied her computer screen. "According to our records, she withdrew twenty-five thousand dollars two months ago."

Morgan clawed at the V-neck of her sweater. That was impossible. "My mother hasn't been anywhere near Harmony Falls in years." At least as far as Morgan knew ... but these days she was so far out of the family loop, anything was possible.

Her father's arrest two weeks ago had come as a complete shock. She'd been the last to know he'd been taking bribes for more than five years, even when he'd been mayor of Harmony Falls. And then last week, out of the blue, her mother and uncle disappeared after being traced to an international flight. Why shouldn't she be the last to know her mother fled the country and cleared out the savings account, too?

"Is there a problem?" A familiar voice came from behind the teller.

Morgan cringed. Mary Kemper, the credit union manager, had been one of Morgan's mother's snobby friends. Mary glanced at Morgan only briefly, and for one blissful second, she thanked the lord for that extra thirty pounds she'd been wearing since Charlotte's birth. But then Mary looked up again.

"Morgan Parrish, is that you?" Her eyes widened as she gasped. "Well, I'm … " Her words tapered off as the shock faded, and her natural arrogance reasserted itself with a cold lift of her chin. "Is there a problem?" she asked again, as if—on second thought—she didn't know Morgan Parrish from "Adam." Probably because the daughter of a felon and a potential fugitive wasn't the most respectable person with whom to conduct small talk.

Well, screw that. Morgan only had twelve more hours in this town, and these days, she had more to worry about than what the country club set wagged their tongues about.

"Hi, Mary. How are you?"

"Fine." How could one word be so painful it wrinkled every ounce of real estate on the woman's face?

The teller tapped a perfectly manicured nail against the screen, speaking in a nervous, hushed whisper. "Ms. Parrish was unaware of the large withdrawal made two months ago."

Mary peered at the screen, and her lips curled. "Well, unfortunately, this account does not require signatures of both account holders for withdrawal. Your mother was within her legal boundaries to withdraw the money." She coughed into her hand.

Legal boundaries? Ha! What about moral boundaries? Her mother didn't seem to care about those. And those indiscretions had Morgan in one hell of a bind. "This is bullshit!"

"I'm sure this is a most unpleasant discovery, Ms. Parrish, but there's no need to make a scene." The woman flashed a fake, tight smile at the customer behind Morgan, then stepped closer and lowered her silky voice to a hiss. "Perhaps your mother decided it was the only way to recoup the money she lost on the wedding after you cheated on the groom. Seems to me *that* started the whole downhill spiral for your family—and this town."

Ouch. Not that she didn't deserve that. But when her daddy had been mayor, nobody would've dared to criticize her. What a difference three years made.

Back then, when Daddy said jump, everyone did. Including her. Agreeing to marry the town's favorite son was the biggest leap of all. Too bad she'd never loved Justin Mitchell as much as her daddy did. If she had, she wouldn't have had sex with her ex—the town's bad boy, Charlie Cramer—the night of her bachelorette party and stupidly left that incriminating tiara in his car for his nosy sister, Alice, to find.

"Oh! *Parrish!*" The teller stared at Morgan with a newfound curiosity. "I never made the connection."

Morgan wished she hadn't, but since she had, there was no use shrinking from the fact. "Yep, Parrish. Kind of like the F-word in these parts now, huh?"

Mary sneered. "You have a lot of nerve being flippant, dear. Your father's in jail. Your mother is God knows where. And that plastics plant your family promised would save this town is only half-built and doomed. Do you know how many people had financial ties to the construction alone?"

"My father," the teller interjected. "He was contracted to do electrical work. He had to layoff half his crew when the plant construction stopped."

Some of the other tellers and customers moved closer and all of them were side-eyeing this conversation. Morgan chewed the inside of her cheek. Gossip at the country club was one thing, but she didn't want anyone breaking out pitchforks and torches. Besides, she wasn't proud of the damage her family had caused. It was just that being flippant felt better than being scared and sad.

Morgan held up her hands in a mea culpa. "Look, I'm sorry about your father. Frankly, I'm sorry about mine, too. There were a lot of victims to his schemes." *I should know.* "I don't condone anything he did, and I wasn't a part of it."

The man in line behind her scoffed. "Aren't you legal counsel for your uncle's corrupt corporation?"

She sighed. "No. I never took that job. I'm not even practicing law anymore." She'd been fired for taking too much time off when Charlotte had gotten sick with all those recurring ear infections. Which was why she'd needed this money. Without it, she wasn't sure what came next.

Knowing when the fight was lost, Morgan turned and simply walked out of the bank.

It wasn't until she was settling back behind the wheel of the Jaguar her daddy'd bought her as a law school graduation present, staring at the beyond-empty gas gauge, that she let her fate sink in.

She was doomed—payback for lying to Justin, cheating with Charlie, and the general self-absorbed bitchiness she'd spread around town before she left.

Karma sucked.

Please, tell me we're even now. "Please," she whispered as she glanced at the sky. How was she ever going to move on with her life if she kept getting dragged back down?

Her answer was a big fat splat on her windshield, courtesy of a low-flying pigeon.

Straightening her wilted posture on a deep breath, Morgan glanced in the rearview mirror at the empty car seat. She needed to get back to Charlotte. Aunt Phyllis was a stranger to the toddler, and that house—Morgan cringed—was barely fit for the cats let alone a two-year-old.

She probably should have taken Charlotte with her—a lady with a baby got more sympathy, at least—but she couldn't risk anyone seeing Charlotte until Charlie knew about the little girl.

Morgan dropped her head to the steering wheel and moaned. This was not how things were supposed to go. She was *supposed* to lay low at Aunt Phyllis's for a couple days, withdraw the money from the savings account, beg for Charlie's forgiveness, so her conscience would quiet, and decide where to go next. What was she supposed to do now? Extend her stay at Aunt Phyllis's?

Living in Hell would be happier for a Parrish than living in Harmony Falls.

The angry red service engine light popped on again, taunting her.

Considering Morgan hadn't kept up with regular maintenance on the car, she'd be lucky if she could make it out of town, even if she had someplace else to go. Whatever was causing the engine light to glow would certainly eat up most—if not all—of the measly thousand dollars that remained from selling off almost everything she'd owned.

She slammed the heel of her hand against the steering wheel, giving it a violent shake. *Stupid car.* She couldn't even afford to take care of it anymore. She should've sold it to the senior partner at the law firm when he'd offered to buy it.

Morgan's eyes widened. Wait a minute. Maybe she could still sell it. If Bryce Becker over at Becker's Car and Truck would buy the Jag for, say, $25,000, then Morgan could buy a newer, cheaper car and pocket the rest. Hell, if she could walk away with $10,000 after unloading this car and buying a new one, she'd still have enough to sign a lease on a small apartment somewhere far away from this town and her family's unfolding legal drama.

Hope was not lost, yet.

But it sure did start to slip ten minutes later when Bryce glared at her from across the used car lot. "Well, looky here. A fox has returned to the hen house." He hiked the shiny black belt holding up baggy dress pants over his beer belly. "I'm surprised a Parrish has the guts to show up in this town again."

Here we go. "It's nice to see you, too." They'd been friends once. Even went to a homecoming dance freshman year.

"I wish I could say the same, I do. But your daddy screwed us over good. Promising to get that plastics plant and all them jobs for us. Said he'd do more as a congressman than Justin Mitchell ever did, and he'd take Harmony Falls along for the ride." Bryce snickered. "Well, he took us for a ride, alright. All the way to prison."

She gritted her teeth. "I don't agree with what my father did." She didn't even know the details. Their relationship had become irreparable the minute she refused to beg Justin to go through with the wedding. "In fact, I haven't spoken to him since I left Harmony Falls."

"And yet, here you are, still behind the wheel of Daddy's fancy car."

"Actually, I want to sell it." *I have to sell it.* But it was never good to show desperation on a used car lot.

Bryce's bushy eyebrows rose. "Is that so?"

He stalked the vehicle. When he peered into the backseat, Charlotte's car seat seemed to glow like a homing beacon. *Crap.* She should've talked to Charlie before she went to the bank. The last thing she needed was some townie running off to tell him Morgan was here ... with a child when he'd spent the last two years thinking she'd placed their baby for adoption.

She bit into her bottom lip as Bryce's eyebrows rose.

"You got yourself a little one, huh?"

Morgan nodded but refused to take the bait.

"You know, Justin's the mayor now, happily married to Alice Cramer." He kept his beady little eyes on the car, opening the driver's side door and plopping onto the seat. "And uh, your other *old pal* Charlie Cramer runs a fancy restaurant in town." He cut his gaze to her, and it was equal parts suspicion and expectation. "You stay in touch with any of them?"

He was fishing for information about the car seat, wasn't he?

The sweat dripping down her back had nothing to do with the warmer-than-usual May temperature. Three years ago, she'd stood on Charlie's front porch and announced her pregnancy just days after Justin had left her at the altar. Alice, Charlie's sister, had always held a torch for Justin and animosity that Morgan seemingly stood in their way. Man, what a convoluted mess their lives must've been for anyone on the outside looking in—and there were a lot of curious people in Harmony Falls. The minute those people got wind of Charlotte, the speculation would begin. *Is she Justin's? Is she Charlie's?*

Morgan couldn't blame them for that. She'd been a spoiled, unhappy young woman, wanting it all and used to getting what she wanted. And she'd wanted Charlie Cramer, even if she already had Justin Mitchell. Her fiancé's congressional schedule put him in Washington for weeks at a time paving the way back to Charlie's backseat for a handful of desperate transgressions exactly nine months prior to Charlotte's arrival

"I haven't stayed in touch with anyone," she said. "I've been busy." First, hiding the pregnancy from her father and mother, who would've pressured her into an abortion had they known she was pregnant with the wrong man's baby. Then, raising her little girl with no family support, because her parents deemed their wayward daughter and illegitimate grandchild a liability to dear old dad's political career.

He gave her a shitty grin. "Maybe you'll get to bump into them while you're here."

God, she hoped not. She didn't want to bump into Justin and Alice—ever. And she wanted her visit with Charlie to go as smoothly as possible, a carefully planned operation.

"Can we skip the small talk and get down to business?" she asked.

"I can give you ten grand for the car," he said.

Ten thousand dollars was a far cry from the twenty-five thousand she'd been hoping for. "Is that because the car is really worth that much, or because I'm a Parrish and you want to stick it to me?"

"The engine light is on. The mileage is sky high. The tires are bald. And that's just what I can see. If this vehicle belonged to my mama, she'd be offered ten grand, too." He pushed off the steering wheel and stood beside the car. "Unlike some of us, I'm not in the business of screwing people over."

The jab actually made Morgan feel a bit better. At least she wasn't being cheated. "Okay. I'll take the ten grand, but now I need another car. What's the cheapest reliable vehicle on the lot?"

Bryce put his hands on his hips and puffed out his chest while he scanned the cars. "I can do $9,000 out the door on that red one over there, but not a penny less."

The snub-nosed, boxy-looking economy car paled in comparison to the long, sleek, sexy curves of her Jaguar. She didn't want to drive something that looked like a clown car. She especially didn't want to hand over almost all of the money she'd just made. "Nine thousand dollars for that leaves me with a measly grand." Plus the grand she already had. She might be able to afford first and last months' rent on $2,000, but it wouldn't leave much room for error. "How about $8,000?"

"Now, don't go getting snobby on me. She might not be the prettiest car on the lot, but with factory warranty and low mileage, that there's a gem. I can't just give it away."

He was enjoying this, wasn't he?

When he waved at someone behind them, Morgan cringed, sinking her head into her shoulders. *Please, don't be someone who knows me.* She'd had about all the vitriol she could take for one day.

"Deal or no deal?" he asked.

"Deal." She'd get over the vehicle's ugliness as long as it wouldn't shake apart into a million pieces on the highway or anything. "Let's go to your office so we can get this done."

Once she'd signed on the dotted line, some way, somehow, Morgan Parrish was getting the hell out of Harmony Falls—again.

• • •

Charlie Cramer's pick-up truck guzzled oil the way he used to guzzle Jack.

Or beer. Or any other alcohol that found its way into his hands.

He shook his head as he detoured from Main Street and pulled into Becker Car and Truck, thankful for more than a thousand days of sobriety. He had his dream job as chef at Char-Grilled Bistro. His sister was happily married. Life as a once pitiful, laughable Cramer had taken a damn good turn. *Finally.*

But maybe he'd spoken too soon.

A white Jaguar with Connecticut plates parked on Bryce's lot. Charlie hit the brakes and rubbed his eyes until they burned. Apparently, there was a downside to sobriety—too many dry days caused hallucinations.

It had to be a hallucination, because that looked like Morgan Parrish's car. He had spent the better part of a year in pursuit of that car and its driver.

With hands clenched around the wheel, he drove straight at the figment of his imagination. At the last minute, he chickened out and turned the wheel. What if it was real? What if Morgan Parrish came back to town?

Son of a bitch. When she'd left town with his baby in her belly, after Justin dropped her cold, Charlie had followed. He'd hoped she would give them a chance to be happy together like they'd been that summer between her freshman and sophomore years in college, before her father stepped in and broke them apart.

But once he'd reached her in Connecticut, she'd refused to talk to him except to threaten a restraining order. So he backed down, got sober, and enrolled in culinary school. Then, the baby had been born and he'd received papers to declare paternity. Charlie scratched an itch over his heart. He didn't fight Morgan's wish to place the child for adoption. As a newly recovered alcoholic, he'd been the last person on earth who should've been a father. And Morgan was no prize, either.

He touched the gritty surface of the white car—just to make sure it was real—and then he headed straight for Bryce's office. If she did have the nerve to show her face in this town again, he had a few things to say.

As he weaved through racks of auto parts and man-sized stacks of tires, the soles of Charlie's cowboy boots echoed. He needed oil and then he needed to get to the bistro for dinner prep. He *didn't* need this aggravation. Pushing the Mitchell family to invest in a small restaurant instead of the bakery they'd proposed meant there was a lot riding on his success.

And it'd been slow to come.

"Afternoon, Charlie," Roberta Urlacher called from behind the checkout counter. "What's on the menu this week? More of that veal? Rudy can't stop talking about it."

"No veal. This week I have duck."

She crinkled her nose. "Ew. Duck is slimy and tough."

"Only when it's cooked by someone who shouldn't be cooking it," he said. "Is Bryce in?"

"Bryce is, uh, closing a deal. Can I help you with something?"

"Oil," he said without taking his eyes off Bryce's office door.

"You use a 5w20 in her, right?"

"Yes." He leaned against the counter, wishing it was a bar.

"Be back in a jiff."

A few seconds later, Charlie heard a door click open and the words, "Good luck to you."

He met Bryce's wide eyes as the man exited his office with a woman behind him. Charlie's heart hammered against his rib cage. She wore her dark hair in a ponytail—something Morgan never did—and the baggy sweatshirt was wrong, too. But he'd have known that face anywhere.

Her mouth opened when she saw him. Maybe his did, too. He was so numb he couldn't feel a damn thing except the vicious thrashing in his chest.

"Well, well, Charlie Cramer, isn't this a surprise?" Bryce grinned. "I'll be right with you."

Morgan stepped toward Charlie, looking different enough he couldn't help but stare. It took him a few seconds to realize she wasn't wearing makeup—not a stitch. For a woman who used to leave smudges of color on his white T-shirts after a hug, it was a shocking change. Was she sick? He used to pray she'd pay for agreeing to that wedding her father wanted and choosing Justin over him, then leaving town the minute they actually got their chance to be together. But he didn't want her to be ill.

"Charlie," she rasped. "I'm … " her mouth closed, and he watched the muscles of her throat move as she swallowed, "visiting my aunt."

Which was weird, too. The high and mighty Parrishes had stayed far away from Kitty's reclusive sister, Phyllis.

"5w20," Roberta said. Her voice ended in a whoop, and the plastic container thudded loudly on the counter.

He might have things to say to Morgan, but he wasn't going to say them here in front of an eager audience.

Reaching into his back pocket, he grabbed his wallet and tossed a twenty onto the counter. "Thanks, Roberta."

"I'm going to call you," Morgan said.

Charlie clenched his jaw. *Two years too late.* He gave Morgan a curt nod but otherwise stood stock still until she and Bryce left the building.

"I should've warned you." Roberta handed him his change. "I was hoping they'd stay in the office long enough for you to get out without seeing her. It must be hard. Is that the first time you've seen her since she left town? "

Charlie's nostrils flared. He didn't like to share details about his life or talk about his feelings with people close to him. He sure as hell wasn't going down that road with an auto parts store cashier. *Small towns.* These people needed to mind their own business.

A growl caught in the back of his throat as he retreated.

It wasn't until he stepped out of the building, clutching the quart of oil, that his head cleared enough to go on the attack again. *Phone call, my ass.* He wasn't waiting around to hear from her.

Charlie jumped into his truck and headed for Phyllis Marion's farmhouse. They had unfinished business.

Chapter Two

After running into Charlie at Becker's Car and Truck, the truth was clear: Karma wasn't done with Morgan yet.

At least there's no engine light haunting me, she thought as she glanced at the gauges of her new car. *Focus on the positive.* It had gotten her through a lot these last three years. Hopefully, it would get her through seeing Charlie again.

He probably hated her. He'd barely said anything. He'd looked like he wanted to pick her up and throw her back to Connecticut with one good heave ho. He'd also looked … wonderful. Better than he'd looked when she'd left. Strong, healthy, rough, and rugged. Like he'd looked in high school. Before the booze became a problem.

She glanced at the rearview mirror and caught sight of Charlotte's car seat. God, what was he going to say—and do—when he found out about the baby? And now she didn't have the money she needed to get out of town and start over after she dropped that nuclear bomb.

Maybe her mother would turn up, and she could get some of the money back. She snorted. *Dream on.* Her mother and Uncle Harold were probably off spending every last dime on umbrella drinks in some luxurious tropical location. This was a woman who'd seen her only granddaughter once in a moment of sentimental weakness. But the minute she'd realized the child bore a strong resemblance to the unfavorable Cramer family, she never attempted to visit again.

It was sad, but she couldn't wallow. She had a daughter to worry about now. And the only way that child was going to have a decent life was if Morgan got a job far away from this town. She could use Aunt Phyllis's address and phone number on applications, but there wasn't an internet connection at the dilapidated farmhouse. It was downright painful searching for jobs and applying on a four-inch screen. Besides, she couldn't get too reliant on her phone. Any day now, she was going to be cut off after two months of not paying the bill.

Maybe she could do this the old-fashioned way.

She still wasn't sure where she should head next, but New York was the nearest major city. The mini-mart was the only place in town to buy the *New York Times,* but they didn't have it. They had Pittsburgh newspapers, though. Pittsburgh was a little too close to Harmony Falls, but she was desperate for a paycheck.

Her gaze locked on the *Pittsburgh Review* and the words *Former Congressman to Be Indicted.*

Bile burned her throat. Right beside the *Review,* the *Gazette* proclaimed: *Bribery, Fraud Among Charges Levied Against Fallen Congressman.* That one had a photo of her father wearing a particularly unflattering sneer.

She grabbed the *Review.* At least with this one, she wouldn't have to see her father staring back at her.

Holding the paper against her chest, she stood in line with her gaze glued to the speckled floor. The kid behind the register was too young to know her, but even so, she had the exact change counted and ready. She wasn't looking for any more conversation today.

As she headed out the door toward the safety of her car, a voice startled her.

"Well, I'll be … " Ginger Abbot's mousy brown hair had been dyed red and cut short and chic, but the splattering of freckles across her wide nose were exactly the same as they'd been in high school. She looked stylish and a lot surer of herself than she'd been all those years ago.

"You look great," Morgan said, clutching the paper tighter to her chest, feeling uncomfortable and a bit jealous.

Ginger sniffed, and the spring air around them chilled at least twenty degrees. "So you *do* remember me?"

Morgan nodded. She just wanted to sprint to her car and lock herself in.

"I find that so odd, considering you ignored me for years. Really, since you told me in eighth grade that we couldn't be friends because my daddy didn't have a job."

Oh, God. She'd said that. She couldn't recall the exact scenario, but the words sounded like something she would've said in the heyday of Parrish rule. Her father had made no bones about his dislike of unemployed people who contributed to statistics that marred his mayoral term.

Morgan squared her shoulders. "Ginger, I … "

"Sorry. I can't be friends with someone whose daddy is in prison."

Burned. And in this case, Morgan deserved it. "I shouldn't have said what I said all those years ago." Surely they could forgive and forget something that was almost two decades old.

Ginger wrinkled her nose. "No, you shouldn't have, but you did, and you never regretted it until you were on the other side, did you? You'll have to forgive me for not feeling very sympathetic, now. I just don't think a tiger can change her stripes." She scanned Morgan from head to toe, zeroing in on the peanut butter Charlotte smudged along her hemline. "Looks like you and your family finally got what you deserved."

Ginger disappeared into the mini-mart and Morgan sighed. She had to get out of here.

She speed-walked to her car, locked the doors, and tore the paper apart until she found the classifieds. With pen in hand, she circled three possibilities. All three were law-related—the only thing she was qualified to do. She wasn't licensed in Pennsylvania, but maybe she could get hired as a paralegal or a law secretary. Though having the same last name as the embattled congressman wouldn't get her in the door for many interviews. The pay would be less than what she was used to as well, which wouldn't make it easy to afford daycare and a decent place to live, but what was the alternative?

Fired or not, she probably should've filed for unemployment. Then at least she would've had a cushion. Diapers weren't cheap. And it could take weeks until she heard back from one of these jobs in Pittsburgh.

No, she didn't have the luxury of being picky and choosy as far as income went.

Five minutes later, she walked into the only law office in Harmony Falls. Heinrich Clark had been a close family friend, but Morgan wasn't under any illusion he'd be happy to see her. This was a longshot at best.

A bell over the door announced her entrance, and Heinrich glanced up from his laptop. "Good after … " He blinked, and his mouth shut.

"Good afternoon, Mr. Clark." She reached a hand over his desk, hoping to keep things as professional as possible despite her sweatshirt and ponytail.

He blinked again, shook her hand, and then stood. "Morgan Parrish. I never thought I'd see you around town again."

"I never thought I'd be here." She offered a nervous laugh and a shrug. "But if these last few years have taught me anything it's to expect the unexpected."

"Sit." He motioned to an empty chair. "Can I get you a cup of coffee?"

Holy hell, he wasn't going to throw her out? She smiled. "Thank you, but no. No coffee. What I could use is a temporary job."

His eyes bulged.

"I can be your paralegal. I can file and answer phones. I just need a paycheck, Mr. Clark, until I can find a permanent job somewhere out of town."

He sat in the nearest chair. "Your mother didn't give you the money from the credit union account, did she? I told her that was the right thing to do."

On second thought … Morgan fell into the chair beside her. "You talked to my mother?"

"A couple weeks ago, shortly after your father's arrest. She called with some legal questions."

That was around the last time Morgan had spoken to her, too. "What legal questions?"

"Morgan, I can't. You know I can't."

"Why not? She's not your client. She's just your friend. I'm her daughter—the daughter she stole from! I have a right to know where she is. I want my money back."

"I don't where she is. The call came up on caller ID as blocked."

"She's with my Uncle Harold isn't she? He's missing, too."

"I don't know."

"Well, *I* know. Our last conversation, she told me spousal privilege should protect her where my father is concerned, but she'd rather die than say something that could incriminate Uncle Harold. They ran off together so he wouldn't get arrested and she wouldn't have to testify!"

"You're speculating."

"What else am I supposed to do? I've been completely in the dark about how rotten my family really is." Which wasn't really a bad thing considering the strained and limited communication over the last three years meant she'd kept her nose clean and her conscience guilt-free as far as the bribery charges were concerned. "She told me she didn't have anything to do with this, but if that's true, then what could she possibly know that could hurt Uncle Harold?"

"I'm sorry."

Morgan used to be sorry about it, too. Now, she was angry. "Forget it. But if you talk to her again, tell her I'm stuck in Hell, I mean, Harmony Falls thanks to her."

"I wish there was something I could do to help you, but I barely have enough cases to keep myself afloat."

"Don't worry about it." Working for her mother's confidant wasn't all that appealing. After all, she wanted to get away from the legal drama, not be smack dab in the middle of it. But hey, at least he hadn't thrown her out or taken potshots like the rest of this town would have done. That was a warped kind of progress.

As she drove down Main Street in search of her next move, a huge white house with paint chipping off its stately decorative pillars mocked her from the passenger side window. Her house. At least, it *had* been her house. She didn't know who owned it now. By the looks of the overgrown shrubbery it could've been vacant. God knew how emotionally vacant it was when she'd lived there. Nothing and nobody mattered but her father's political pursuits.

She thought of him again when she passed the mayor's office, where she used to sit across from him as a child and listen to his plans for political domination. Later, when she was an adult, he became convinced that Justin, the Mitchells' golden child, would lead them straight to Pennsylvania Avenue. The minute her father had been successful in breaking her and Charlie apart, he'd started talking about Morgan as the perfect well-educated, polished first lady. By the time law school began, she'd gotten caught up in the power and the plans, too. She glanced down at her sweatshirt and laughed. Boy, did plans change. She was a wreck, at the moment, and Justin walked away from Congress for a quiet life as mayor.

Justin. Her eyes widened. He ran this town. Surely he could help her out with temporary employment. After all, he'd want her gone faster than anyone else.

Before nerves took hold and froze her in place, she thought about Charlotte. She'd have faced worse for her. So, she tightened her ponytail and marched into the municipal building.

The woman behind the reception desk gasped. Agnes Chase. Only in a town this small would the mayor's staff remain intact after a change in leadership.

"Hi, Agnes," Morgan said, lifting her hand in a lilting wave, feeling like a little girl again only with much less exuberance.

"Morgan," Agnes breathed, oozing pure shock.

"Yep. I'm back. Is Justin available?"

Agnes leapt from her chair. "He is … " she blocked the door, "but he's busy."

Three years apart and a marriage couldn't keep these people from wanting to protect their precious Justin from the claws of Morgan Parrish. "I'm not here to cause trouble." She rested a hand over her heart. "I promise. I just have nowhere else to turn."

Agnes looked at the ceiling as if she expected the word of God to guide her next move.

Justin opened the door instead.

"Holy shit," he said in a very un-mayor-like way that would've made Morgan laugh under different circumstances. "I heard … I thought … "

"I was trying to send her away," Agnes stammered right along with him.

"I'm not here to cause trouble," Morgan said again.

Justin stared at her. His narrow-eyed scrutiny made it hard to swallow. She'd felt the same tightness at the church on their wedding day, after he'd found out she'd been carrying on with Charlie.

"It's okay, Agnes. This won't take long." He patted the older woman's shoulder, nudging her aside. "Right this way, Ms. Parrish."

When Justin didn't close the door behind them, Morgan allowed herself a small smile. He was no dummy. Without a witness, this town would go crazy wondering what had transpired in this room.

"What can I do for you?" His tone was even-keeled and all business, as if Morgan walking into his office was just another blip in a mundane day.

Meanwhile, her stomach was turning inside out.

She scanned the office that looked much the same as it did when her daddy had been here. Blue carpeting, dark paneling, big cherry desk. She shouldn't have come. Too many memories. But she needed a job. Suddenly, it seemed laughable and terribly presumptuous of her to expect Justin to help her. "I'm sorry." *For interrupting your day*, but the minute she said the first two words she realized she'd never apologized for giving him a reason to leave her at the altar in the first place. That was most definitely the right place to start. "I behaved badly while we were engaged— very badly."

He nodded, but there wasn't a crack in his business-like veneer.

"At almost thirty years old, I should've known better and been stronger, but obviously I wasn't. I still had a lot of growing up to do. That's not an excuse, and I don't expect you to forgive me … "

"Good," he cut in, his brows finally dipping low enough to show some emotion. "I don't think I can. You betrayed me. And you betrayed this town."

Yes, she had done those things, but she couldn't change them, now. Even if she could, she wouldn't—if it meant losing Charlotte. She had a feeling Justin could relate. "I know, and I'm sorry I hurt people, but three years later can't we say some good came from it? You're mayor. You have Alice. If we would have kept our promise to our parents—to *this town*—you would've been tied to a woman you didn't love. And you might've gotten caught up in my father's scandal. Isn't where you are now better?"

He scowled. "Where I am now doesn't change the fact you cheated on me! And humiliated me! Three years isn't enough time to make me forget how that feels."

He glanced at the open door, and she imagined Agnes's ears trained on every word.

"You didn't deserve that," Morgan said. He'd been driven and emotionally distant like her father the entire two years they'd dated, but it didn't raise enough of a red flag to stop her from crawling into his bed or saying yes to his proposal. She'd had no right to humiliate him. "I wish I had handled things differently." A lot of things. Things with Charlie, especially.

He stared at her for a moment, until his expression grew inscrutable. Finally he blinked, and looked back down at the papers on his desk. "If that's all, I have work to do."

The politically poised, emotionally robotic man returned. That was what her parents had wanted her to be, too. She looked down at the peanut butter smudged on the hem of her sweatshirt.

"Actually, there was something else." God, did she really have the nerve to do this? Then again, was there another choice? Charlotte needed fed and a roof over her head. "I need a job," she blurted before she lost her nerve.

Justin's brows shot high on his forehead and she expected him to swear again. "Are you kidding me?"

"Nothing permanent. I won't stay long, I promise."

"You have a lot of nerve." He shook his head. "I can't hire you. First of all, we have all the legal counsel we need."

"It doesn't have to be law-related. I just need a paycheck."

He jammed a hand through his hair and huffed. "It's not going to happen. I don't trust you enough to hire you. And even if I did, Alice would never be comfortable with you working here. I don't know why you thought it was a good idea to come back to Harmony Falls."

Morgan had only one excuse, and she was worth it. "I have my reasons."

There was nothing else to say after that, so she left, nearly walking right by the bright red clown car. She didn't even recognize her life anymore. It would've been enough to crush her spirit if there wasn't a little girl with cherub cheeks and bouncy blonde curls waiting for her at Aunt Phyllis's house.

• • •

Charlie stomped up the crumbled cement steps that led to the front door of the dilapidated farmhouse. A cat with matted fur scurried past him, and Charlie did an awkward sidestep to get out of the way. What the hell was Morgan doing here? Phyllis was crazy. Rumor had it she kept a loaded rifle propped beside the door to chase off anything that didn't have four legs.

Glancing down at his legs, Charlie snarled. He should be chopping onions right now, not chasing after Morgan again. But he needed answers.

Before he could knock, Phyllis cracked the front door. All he could see was one oversized eyeball and a slice of wrinkled cheek. "Whatever you're selling, I'm not buying."

"I'm not selling anything. Where's Morgan?"

"Not here." She started to close the door.

Charlie stuck the tip of his cowboy boot in the crack. "I saw her in town, and she said she was visiting you. She also said we needed to talk. Well, I'm here ... " he wedged his foot deeper, "to talk."

"I told you. She's not here." Phyllis slammed the door against his foot.

Damn it! Charlie jumped back, and the door closed.

A sane man would walk away. Hell, he'd walked away from Morgan before, but Charlie wasn't sane. Sober was all he could handle.

He knocked, but Phyllis didn't answer. He knocked again, and she yelled, "Get off my property!"

"Charlie!" In the ruckus with Phyllis, he hadn't heard Morgan pulling into the dirt drive. She ran toward him, red-faced and breathless. "What are you doing here?"

Confronting the bitch who broke my heart. But he didn't say it, because that was pathetic. He was done with pathetic. "I figured I'd save you the phone call," he said instead. "Turns out I have some things to say to you, too."

Her gaze flashed toward the house and then back to him again. "Fine! Say them. But out here. She doesn't need to hear this."

He looked back at the house, expecting to see Phyllis brandishing a rifle. That damn cat glared at him from the top step. "Why in God's name *are* you here?"

"I'm just visiting."

"You're paying a friendly visit to a woman you and your family refused to acknowledge while you lived here? I'm not buying it, so let's try this again. Why … are … you … here?" He slowed his words, even though he was out of patience.

She choked on a sob. "I have no place else to go." Her gaze flashed behind him again. "I got fired from my job. When I tried to find another one, nobody would hire me. I'm sure the investigation against my father and his arrest didn't help. Then I fell behind on rent and got evicted. I thought there was some money in an old credit union account, so I came to withdraw it, but my mother beat me to it. She took it all so she could leave the country with my uncle. I'm stuck … in Harmony Falls."

"Fuck."

"There's more."

"No!" He held up his hand. "I don't want to hear any more from you until I've said what I've wanted to say for the last two years."

She stuck out her chin and locked her jaw like she expected the words to pack one hell of a punch.

"I hate what you did," he said. "All of it. I should've told you to go to hell when you broke things off, saying you wanted your daddy to be proud of you, and that meant you couldn't be with me. I should've washed my hands of you then. But no, I let you cry on my shoulder too many damn times, and twice that led to … " he sneered, "other things. Justin and I may have grown apart long before you two got engaged, but I still owed him more respect than that. I owed myself more respect than that. Falling in love with you was the stupidest thing I ever did. No wonder I ended up a drunk. You damn near destroyed me."

Her lip quivered. "I didn't mean to."

"Really?" He fisted his hands and lifted his face to the sky for a roar. "Tell me you would've stopped that wedding had my sister not stood up and stopped it for you."

She opened her mouth but shut it again.

"That's what I thought." He shook his head. "You're sick. But the good news is, I'm not … not anymore. You might be stuck in Harmony Falls, but you better stay the hell away from me."

Her gaze shot to the house again, but this time she gasped.

He turned in time to see Phyllis's head. "Is everything okay? I heard yelling."

"Shut the door!" Morgan's whole body jerked like she was readying to run.

"I can call the cops."

"I said shut the … "

And then a child cried.

Charlie's blood ran cold as Phyllis slammed the door. "Who was that?"

"Nobody." Morgan rushed toward the house. "Leave, Charlie, or I'll call the cops myself."

A child. Whose child? The hairs on the back of his neck stood. "Morgan … "

But she didn't stop, and she slammed the door behind her like Phyllis had done, leaving him gaping in the driveway with the sound of a crying child ringing in his ears.

Damn it! She'd said there was more. Was this part of it?

He jogged to the porch, grabbed hold of the knob and pushed inside.

Morgan spun around at the mouth of the hallway on the far side of the room. "Charlie! You can't just barge in here. I told you to leave."

"Who's that crying?" He could barely get the words out his voice was shaking so badly.

"I … uh … first, you need to calm down."

A muffled cry came from somewhere down the hall, and instinct forced Charlie past her.

"Wait!" She clawed at his biceps.

He lunged for the only closed door, and when he opened it, he came face to face with the child—all three feet of her—standing stock still beside Phyllis's ugly quilt-covered bed. She clutched a pink blanket to her chubby cheek, while one blonde curl hung in her teary eye. She looked like a mini-version of his sister. Her sniffles shot right through him, heating the blood that only seconds ago had turned to ice.

Mine, Charlie thought, but that couldn't be true. Regardless of genetics, he'd signed away his rights. Morgan was supposed to sign away her rights, too. She'd found a family, a pediatrician and a preschool teacher. They were going to give the baby, who got caught up in the Parrish-Mitchell web of lies, a proper life with a backyard and a swing set and trips to Disney World instead of a mother with a warped family allegiance and a father with an alcohol problem.

"Charlotte!" Morgan's shrill voice mixed with the bang of the door as it hit the wall. "It's okay."

The child squealed and lunged toward Morgan, who blew past Charlie without a word.

"Charlotte," she said again but softer as she clutched the little girl. "I'm sorry if we upset you."

Charlotte. Charlie bent at the waist and grabbed just above his knees.

"Everything's okay," Morgan continued to soothe.

Charlie almost called bullshit. It wasn't okay, but he couldn't drag enough air into his lungs to stand up straight, let alone speak.

"Can you give us a minute?" Morgan asked.

Aunt Phyllis nodded, and slipped past him into the hall. "But if I hear yelling again, I'm not going to ask if you're okay; I'm just going to call the cops."

Anger deep and dark built inside him until it straightened his spine. He shook his head. "No need. I'm leaving. I can't do this right now."

"Charlie, we *need* to do this."

He shook his head. "Not in front of … the kid." He didn't trust himself to keep the conversation cordial, and he wasn't sure he could handle hearing the child cry again. Those cries had ripped right through him.

"Fine," Morgan said through gritted teeth. "Then I'll get her settled, and we can talk on the porch. I told you I had more to tell you." She kissed the little girl's head. "Wait for me outside."

He didn't owe her the courtesy, but he sat on the front steps among the curious cats and a few roaming chickens. They looked at him like he had something to give. He had nothing. Seeing Morgan again—with a child—wiped him clean. Emptied him out. He leaned forward with elbows on knees, staring at the worn tips of his boots.

Son of a bitch. He thought he was beyond all this.

Finally, the door creaked behind him, and he stood.

"This is not the way I planned for you to find out."

"Find out *what* exactly?" The burn in his throat worsened with every word. He already knew the answer to that question, but he wanted to hear her say it.

"Charlotte is yours." Shiny, fat tears spilled down her extra pale face.

He winced. It sure as hell wasn't in sympathy.

"I couldn't go through with putting her up for adoption. I was going to tell you. I just didn't know when or how."

"How 'bout calling me the day she was born? 'Charlie, we have a baby girl, and I'm going to keep her,'" he mocked Morgan's voice. "Seems simple as sin to me."

She shook her head. "I called the house, and Alice answered. She said you were finally moving on and sober, and that you'd enrolled in culinary school. So I hung up and decided to wait until I was certain and the timing was better—for both of us. You didn't need me screwing things up with an announcement I wasn't even sure I was ready to make."

Rage put him right in her face. "That wasn't your decision to make."

She stepped back. "Maybe not, but the note you sent along with the paternity papers made me think I'd done the right thing. You said an alcoholic would make a shitty father anyway. Your words. Not mine. I wanted you sober and happy, so I respected your wishes."

"You wanted to make it easy on yourself, so you kept it from me," he spit out.

Her mouth dropped. "You think raising a child on my own is *easy?*"

"I don't know what it's like, because you never told me! If you had, you would've found out I've been clean as a whistle since the day you left Harmony Falls."

"*Because* I left Harmony Falls."

He wasn't going to argue with that. He hadn't started drinking dangerously until she'd left for law school after telling him she couldn't see him again. He wished to god she'd stuck to that plan.

Morgan's shoulders slumped, and the wall around Charlie's heart developed a hairline crack. She looked so sad. For a split second, he itched to hold her.

Luckily, there were three years filled with damn-near hatred keeping his sentimentality in check.

He turned and walked away.

"I understand," she called after him. "I don't expect anything from you. I just wanted you to know."

And he just wanted a drink.

Instead, he was going straight to the restaurant to viciously chop some onions.

Chapter Three

Every time Morgan closed her eyes, she saw Charlie's angry face. Every time she opened her eyes, she saw his nose and his smile— on Charlotte's angelic face. It was a vicious cycle, and she had no idea how to stop it.

But she couldn't leave town with no income, no safe place to go, and a child in tow.

That's why she was standing on the Mitchell's front steps. If anyone in this town was powerful enough to find her a temporary job, it was Justin's mother, Margaret. On the other hand, if anyone in this town had reason to hate a Parrish, it was Margaret, too.

Morgan winced, but she knocked anyway.

Hopefully, three years had been enough time for Margaret to get over her oldest son being made a fool at the altar.

Constance, the Mitchells' housekeeper, answered the door, and a rush of air-conditioned chill greeted Morgan. Constance used to make oatmeal raisin cookies whenever she knew Morgan was coming around back when she was engaged to Justin.

There'd be no baked goods now.

"My, my, my," Constance clucked. "I never would've guessed it'd be you behind that knock."

"Surprise." Morgan managed a tentative smile. "Is Mrs. Mitchell in?"

Constance's brows rose, and her forehead wrinkled. "Right this way." With a sweep of her arm, she stepped to the side, allowing Morgan to pass. "Mrs. Mitchell and Mark are playing Scrabble in the breakfast room."

If Morgan didn't know the Mitchells, she'd be picturing a Normal Rockwell moment to settle her nerves. Instead, she cringed at the image in her head, one that included Margaret cursing at

Mark a second before she flipped the game board and charged the doorway to accost the woman who cheated on her favorite son.

"Pardon the interruption." Constance stepped into the sunny breakfast room off the cavernous kitchen, where stainless steel and stone surfaces gleamed.

The room turned dark the minute Margaret saw Morgan.

"Hello, Mrs. Mitchell. Mark." She nodded at Justin's brother.

"Put the game away, Mark." Margaret didn't take her eyes off Morgan.

When Constance left the room, Morgan almost grabbed the woman's wrist so she couldn't get away. One semi-neutral witness to this conversation would be a comfort.

"Well, don't just stand there gawking," Margaret said. "Get on with it. An apology shouldn't take all day."

That wasn't why Morgan came, but she could see how it would be expected. She hadn't seen the Mitchells since the wedding debacle. Apologizing was a good thing to do—even if she partially blamed Margaret for trying to push her son into a loveless marriage. "I am very sorry for any embarrassment my indiscretions caused you and your family. I handled everything poorly. I put Justin's career in jeopardy. I panicked, because I wasn't strong enough to stand up to my father and tell him marrying Justin wasn't what I wanted to do. No offense to your son, ma'am. He's a wonderful man. He just wasn't the man for me."

Margaret sniffed. "So you cheated on him?"

"I was confused and probably self-sabotaging. I wish I had made better decisions." But then she wouldn't have had Charlotte.

"I hope your don't expect to be forgiven on the merit of some pretty words. About all I can muster for you at the moment is pity."

She'd take it. Maybe it would help her leave this house with a job. She needed a paycheck more than she needed anyone's forgiveness.

"Fortunately, Justin has moved on nicely," Margaret added. "His personal and professional success is helping to keep this conversation cordial. Does he know you're back in town?"

Morgan nodded. "I saw him already. I apologized. I also … asked him for a job, which, of course, he refused to give me."

Margaret's eyes narrowed. "You have a lot of nerve."

"He said the exact same thing, and you're both right. But I'm stuck here until I can save enough money to leave. I need short-term employment. I know that's a tall order considering my reputation and my family's reputation in this town, but I need a job."

"What happened to your job in Connecticut?"

Morgan swallowed her pride. "I got fired."

"And you think I should help someone who's been fired to find new employment when there are plenty of good people in this town who've never been fired, but can't find work either? You're just as spoiled and entitled as you've always been."

Well, when she put it like that it sure did seem so. But she'd changed, and she was still changing, thanks to Charlotte. "I know I'm asking for a lot, but it's not just me I'm asking for. I have a daughter."

Margret shot Mark a tight glance, and he returned the look with a nervous laugh.

Just as Morgan was about to broach the subject of Charlotte's paternity, Constance returned with tea. The traditional show of hospitality didn't offer any comfort. The way things had been going since she'd stepped foot in Harmony Falls, hers was probably poisoned.

Margaret shooed Constance away after the tray had been placed on the table, and then set about pouring. The lid of the china pot rattled as she struggled to fill each cup. Mark didn't offer to help. Morgan didn't dare. A lot could change in three years, but Margaret's independent streak wasn't likely to be among those things.

"Sit."

Let the inquisition begin, Morgan thought, as she followed Margaret's command.

Mark smiled as he pushed the board game aside. It was unexpected, and comforting.

She'd never been particularly close with Mark, even when she'd been engaged to Justin. He was kind of quiet, and he had the oddest sense of humor, not to mention a crazy-strong allegiance to his mother. But he seemed like a good guy.

The sea grass chair crackled beneath her weight as she sat. Margaret slid a cup of tea toward Morgan, and then passed one to Mark.

"Thank you," he said, raising the cup to his lips, but he waited to sip.

"This tea is cold," Margaret said, grimacing as she swallowed. "Constance!"

Morgan sipped hers out of curiosity. Ice cold.

Mark placed his cup on the floral tablecloth and smiled again. "I knew that was coming," he mouthed.

"Another pot, and hot," Margaret commanded when Constance entered the room. "How hard is it to heat tea water to an appropriate serving temperature?"

"Maybe you should fire Constance and hire Morgan as your housekeeper."

Morgan choked on her tea.

Margaret stared at her. "No. Constance's tea skills may be lacking lately, but she can be trusted."

"I deserve that."

"You deserve worse than that, young lady, but lucky for you, I'm a reasonable woman."

Mark laughed, but then Margaret gripped the table, shaking the teacups as her body jerked. The movement was followed by Mark's groan.

She'd kicked him. Morgan hid a chuckle behind her teacup. What an odd visit this was turning out to be.

"Now, tell me about this child," Margaret said.

Morgan set the cup to the table. How much should she tell? Ever since the positive pregnancy test, she'd been excessively protective of Charlotte. But at the very least, they needed to know the little girl wasn't Justin's. "Well, she's two years old, her name is Charlotte … and she's Charlie's."

Margaret seemed to mull that over, pursing her lips and squeezing her hands as they intertwined on the tabletop.

The silence was so nerve-wracking that Morgan had to fill it. "Without a job, I can't stabilize myself enough to leave town and find a suitable place to live and raise her. I want to find a place where we won't be judged by the Parrish name and I can build a life we can be proud of."

Finally, Margaret nodded. "The child changes things. I'm not a heartless woman. If you knew anything about gardening, I would hire you here. The weeds are out of control, but you'd have to be able to tell a weed from a wild flower. Once again, I don't trust you."

It was the first time since she arrived in Harmony Falls that she was happy to be mistrusted. Hunching over Margaret's flower beds with filthy hands and sweat beading down her back while Justin and Alice came and went for family dinners would turn this sojourn in purgatory into a stint in Hell.

"Good help is hard to find," Mark said. Again, he wore the offbeat smile.

Constance returned. Before she could set the steaming pot of tea on the tray in front of Margaret, Mark rose from his chair.

"I'll take that, thank you." He reached for the pot. "And I'll pour, Mother. You go ahead with your conversation."

He poured fresh cups with a steady hand, leaving his mother's less-than-full. Morgan got the feeling the cold tea hadn't been a mistake so much as it was a concession to allow an unsteady Margaret the satisfaction of serving. It was kind of sweet and unexpected in the Mitchell household.

"You know where we need good help?" Margaret asked with one brow lifted. "At the restaurant."

"Mother, Morgan is a lawyer. Don't you think … "

Lawyer or not, she was desperate. "I'll do anything." But preferably something that would keep her out of the line of sight of most people. Like dishwashing. She couldn't imagine the ruckus she'd cause if she were waiting tables at the Mitchell-owned Main Street Diner.

She lifted her warm teacup to her lips and sipped.

"Good. Then it's settled. Stop by and tell Charlie I hired you. It's only fair he helps contribute to the financial longevity of the mother of his child. Maybe he can put you on the tables tonight and chase that one that talks like she has garbage in her mouth out the door."

Morgan choked on the hot liquid. Charlie was cooking at the diner? No. Bryce said he had a fancy restaurant. "I … I thought … well, the diner … "

"No. The diner is fully staffed. It's that God forsaken, over-reaching bistro I'm talking about. It would've been better off a bakery, but what do I know. I got overruled by my own sons, who thought it was a good idea to financially back a talented but temperamental chef. Mutiny."

Mark put up his hands. "Not me. I abstained from the vote."

Was this a joke? Was this Margaret's way of getting back at Morgan for the havoc she'd wreaked on Justin's personal life and political career? Work with Charlie? She might be desperate, but he wasn't, and he would never want her there.

He hadn't even been able to finish their conversation on the porch.

"That's not going to work," Morgan said.

Margaret didn't flinch. "That's all I have."

Then this visit had been a colossal waste of time. She stood. "I'm sorry for bothering you. Thank you for the tea."

When Morgan was three steps from the front door, she heard Mark call out, "Wait."

She stopped with her hand on the doorknob. "Why? So your mother can entertain herself by watching me beg and squirm some more? No, thanks. I get it, Mark. I screwed up. I made terrible decisions, and I'm going to pay for them for the rest of my life. Payback's a bitch and all that, but even I have some pride. I'm just trying to claw my way out of the mess I made. I realize that's going to be damn near impossible in this town."

He frowned. "Mother wasn't kidding. Jobs are hard to come by around here. And despite that, we can't seem to keep the bistro fully staffed. Charlie's food is wonderful, but he's a control freak and moody as hell. Most people don't want to put up with that. But you, on the other hand, have a vested interest in his success what with Charlotte being your top concern. Wouldn't it be nice for her father's restaurant to be stable and lucrative?" His brows knitted together, and for a second, she saw a sincerity that bore a similarity to Justin.

"Why are you being nice to me?"

Mark shrugged. "I always root for the outcasts."

There was no way Charlie would agree to this. Yesterday, he told her she'd almost destroyed him—and that was *before* he found out about Charlotte. God only knew what sort of shape he was in today.

She staved off a shudder with a shake of her head. "Thanks, Mark, but I think it's a bad idea. If you hear of any other jobs, will you let me know?"

Charlie's bistro was the last place on earth Morgan would ever work.

• • •

"Charlie, it's Will."

Charlie leaned the sledgehammer against the wall and reached for a water bottle on the mantle. "Hey, Will. What's up?"

"I've got some bad news. Amy quit."

He closed his eyes and took a good long drink. "When? I just saw her last night and she didn't say anything to me."

"She called me about five minutes ago. She was scared you would yell at her."

Like he'd yelled at her last night when she'd backed into the refrigerator and dropped a plate of ravioli. What was he supposed to do? Hug her? There was a reason for the saying, "If you can't stand the heat, get out of the kitchen."

"Hannah can wait tables with Corbin. I don't need a hostess."

"Corbin was hired to be your assistant chef. How long do you think he'll stay if he's only waiting tables?"

Charlie chucked the water bottle across the empty room. Why were people so goddamned sensitive? "Listen, I'll call Amy and apologize."

"I'm not sure that's such a good idea. She was pretty upset. I have a couple applications on my desk. I'll take a look at them first thing tomorrow and see if I can get someone in there by end of week."

He didn't know what was worse, running short staffed or having to train people over and over again. If only he could learn to keep his mouth shut.

It was so much harder without alcohol taking the edge off his emotions.

"Thanks, Will."

"You're welcome, Charlie. But you've got to cut me a break. My mother is ready to pull financial support and open a bakery instead. I can only hold her off so long if the place isn't turning a profit, and right now, it's not. Expenses are far exceeding income. Now, the food is great, and we've done our best to keep prices competitive, so the bad publicity from the carousel of wait staff must be keeping people away. Someway, somehow, you've got to find a way to get people into that restaurant and keep them there."

Charlie nodded. If he had to have his mouth wired shut, he would. That bistro was a part of him. It was his idea, his décor, his menu, and he'd invested all of the money he'd ever saved in a measly twenty-percent share just so he could say he owned a piece of it.

Once the call ended, he drove his finger into the volume button on the wireless speaker on the mantle, filling the dusty living room of his childhood home with country music. He had a gourmet kitchen to finish.

The sledgehammer made short work of the papier-mache-like drywall between the living room and breakfast nook. A few more days off, and he could move the appliances—a six-burner stove, double ovens, and catering fridge—from the garage into the kitchen. That would be a milestone in the renovation that began when Alice moved in with Justin.

For some reason, thinking about them was a direct pass to thinking about Morgan … and Charlotte.

His chest contracted, and the sharp pain made him swing off balance, sending the sledgehammer into the floor. The wood planks shook from the blow, and one loose board lifted. Before Charlie could pound it back into place with a stomp of his boot, he saw something glistening.

He dropped to his knees, pulled back three additional loose floorboards, and discovered a stockpile of liquor covered in soot. Like a sunken treasure.

"Dad, you're killing me." Charlie dropped his butt to the heels of his boots and lifted his face to the ceiling.

The old man had unsuccessfully kicked the habit thousands of times before liver failure made sure he'd never drink again. Alice had thought she'd rid the house of his stashes. Who'd have thought to look under the floor?

Charlie lifted the full, filthy bottles from their tomb and lined them up on the mantle while Zac Brown Band sang about cold beer on a Friday night. It was Sunday, and there wasn't any beer in the house, but there was liquor—enough to make Charlie forget the shit storm that was brewing beyond his front door. Between Morgan and Charlotte being in town, and the warning from Will, today was not the day Charlie needed to find liquor … unless he was looking to test his sobriety.

He traced a finger over the black label—turned gray from years of dust. The grime coated his finger as he imagined the heated sensation of the liquid coating his throat and numbing his heart. But the barrier would be temporary. The buzz would wear off, and he'd feel worse afterwards.

Still, he lifted the bottle off the mantle and carried it with him to the kitchen like he was in a trance. With a growl, he untwisted the cap and poured two fingers worth of copper-colored liquid into a juice glass.

He stared at it. His mouth watered. This was the closest he'd been to alcohol in years. But no matter how badly he wanted the drink to dull the emotions, the loudest voice in his head screamed, "Dump it."

He really was over that dark part of his life, wasn't he?

"Charlie, we have to talk."

Alice. Charlie spilled the whiskey in the sink, but he didn't have time to hide the bottle.

"What are you doing?" She gasped and then covered her mouth a second before she lunged for the bottle and shattered it against the porcelain.

"Jesus, Alice!" He grabbed her as he jumped clear of the spraying glass and liquor.

"Don't 'Jesus, Alice' me." She drove fists into his chest. "Are you crazy?"

"I didn't drink it."

"Why do you have it?" Her face turned splotchy as tears ran down her cheeks.

"Alice … " Charlie gripped her by the upper arms and shook her, hoping to calm her down, "I found it under the floor boards. It was his. Not mine."

"Then why was it open?"

He let her go and dropped into a kitchen chair. "I don't know. I guess I was testing myself before I dumped it."

She screamed. "Of all the stupid, ridiculous, terrible things to do … "

"Morgan is back."

"I know." She knelt beside him, rubbing a hand atop his knee. "Justin told me, a day late, and I'm not happy about that, but he told me."

"She has the baby," he whispered. "My baby."

Alice's eyes popped wide. "But I thought … "

"She couldn't go through with it."

"Oh, Charlie." She threw her arms around his neck and buried her face in his chest.

He sat there frozen, wondering if he could've handled the smallest drink—just to smooth out the edges.

"You're a dad."

He nodded.

She let go of him and stood. "I'm going to dump that booze, and then we're going to talk."

He supposed that was for the best. No matter how loud the wise voice in his head, why tempt fate? He was an alcoholic who shouldn't be keeping company with his father's stash. He was also a father who needed to do right by his little girl.

After this talk with Alice, he was going to figure out what his rights were as far as Charlotte was concerned, and then he was going to see her again.

Chapter Four

Oh, God, why is she crying? Why won't she fall asleep?

Morgan stilled beneath the covers in her aunt's guest bed, hoping the child beside her would settle. Charlotte had been awake and crying for four of the last six hours.

"Shh." Morgan scooted closer to Charlotte. This had been hard on her angel, too. "Shh," she said again. "It's okay. Mommy's here."

She brushed her lips across Charlotte's forehead. Her skin was scorching. *Crap.* No wonder the child was miserable; she was sick. Again.

"Need help?" Aunt Phyllis stood in the dim light of the hallway.

"Thanks, but I'm not sure there's anything you can do, not unless you have children's pain reliever."

"I had a chicken break a leg not too long ago. I treated her with children's pain reliever. There might be some left. Let me check."

Morgan blinked against the darkness and held Charlotte closer. Thank God for Aunt Phyllis's eccentricities. Her mother used to rant about how Phyllis had lost her mind, but after three days of being here, Morgan had realized her aunt was more quirky than crazy, and she was eager to help. She was the only one Morgan could count on. Having someone—anyone—felt good.

After a dose of medicine and several minutes in the rocking chair, Charlotte fell asleep draped across Morgan's body.

Aunt Phyllis sat on the couch across from them, having refused to go back to bed. Two cats cuddled beside her. "She needs to see a doctor."

"I know." Morgan pushed her feet off the floor, setting the chair rocking. "When she pulls on her ear like that, it always means an ear infection. She needs an antibiotic. But I don't have insurance." She couldn't afford to extend the policy after she'd been fired.

It was another reason she needed to find work fast.

"Kory Flemming took a look at my chicken even though she's not a vet. Ask her."

Alice's best friend who'd left town years ago? Maybe Aunt Phyllis was crazy after all. "Isn't Kory in Chicago?"

Aunt Phyllis made a face. "No. She's engaged to Will Mitchell and splitting time between the nursing home and Valley Hospital."

This town. Even those with the brightest futures couldn't seem to stay away. Harmony Falls sucked them right back in. "Let's see how she's doing in the morning."

With any luck the worst would have passed.

Come morning, Charlotte's fever was back with a vengeance, and Morgan swallowed her pride. Again.

"Mitchell residence. This is Constance speaking. How may I help you?"

"Hello, Constance. This is Morgan…" Her last name caught in her throat, something that had been happening ever since her father's arrest. "Is Mark available?"

"One moment, please."

By the time Mark said hello, Charlotte was screaming again. Morgan bounced the child on her knee until Aunt Phyllis came inside from feeding the chickens, washed her hands, and scooped up the miserable girl.

"Wow. Somebody has a set of lungs," Mark said.

"Charlotte is sick, and I need an antibiotic called in for her. I don't have insurance, but I do have some money. Do you think … would you ask … Kory if she'd help me out?"

Morgan's chest convulsed. Being desperate and needy sucked, but seeing Charlotte in pain was worse.

"I can ask."

"Thank you."

"I'll let you know as soon as I've talked to her."

"Thank you," she said again, letting relief soothe some of the worry.

An hour later, it was back as she sat in Aunt Phyllis's living room, watching Kory Flemming stick an otoscope in Charlotte's ear.

"Poor, baby," Kory said. "It's a mess in there." She gave a pointed look at Morgan, who had filled her in on Charlotte's medical history. "She needs to see a pediatrician for long-term treatment of this. If they're recurring at this rate, there are things that can be done."

"As soon as I find a job and get some health insurance, I'm on it."

"You shouldn't wait that long." Kory pulled a prescription pad from the front pocket of her black satchel. "Get her on medical assistance or state aid."

Morgan winced. How many times had her father complained about people who took handouts? But Kory was right; Charlotte needed to see a pediatrician.

"I'll check into it."

"You do that." Kory held out the prescription. "There are programs for you as well. Look into WIC."

This wasn't happening. She had a law degree. Women with law degrees weren't homeless. They didn't apply for public assistance.

Then Charlotte stirred in her arms, her small face twisted up in pain. Tomorrow morning, she was going to drive to Rileyville and walk into every law firm in that mid-sized town—and then, she would find a daycare for Charlotte, where hopefully the little one would be healthier than she had been in Connecticut.

After Kory had gone, Charlotte fell asleep on Morgan's chest. She needed to get to the pharmacy before it closed, but every time she tried to pass the little one off to Aunt Phyllis, she woke screaming.

"I can go." Aunt Phyllis stifled a yawn. "That Impala might not be pretty, but she still knows the way to town."

Morgan smiled. Thank God for Aunt Phyllis. She didn't seem to mind the chaos Morgan and Charlotte brought to her quiet life. But Morgan wasn't going to take advantage of that. "Thank you, but you need to go lay down. We all need some sleep after last night. I can take her with me. She'll sleep the whole way there." Hopefully.

Aunt Phyllis shuffled off to her bedroom, kittens scurrying behind her just as Morgan closed her eyes. She would enjoy a little peace and quiet before she attempted the trip to town.

Her breathing barely had time to even before a knock on the front door rattled her. Charlotte cried. She carried the child to the window and peeked around the curtains.

Charlie.

So much for peace and quiet.

* * *

Focus on the child. That's why he was back on Phyllis's front porch after he'd told Morgan to stay the hell away from him. Whatever had happened between him and her didn't matter anymore. No matter how much he hated what she'd done and the fact that she was in Harmony Falls again, she was here … with his daughter. He needed to keep a lid on his anger.

Maybe he wasn't cut out to be a father, but he had a right to know for sure.

The door opened, and Morgan stared at him. "I didn't expect to see you again." Her eyes were rimmed in red, and her hair was falling out of its ponytail.

"Yeah, well, I had some time to calm down." But still his jaw clenched. This woman was going to screw up his life again, wasn't she? "We should talk about … the kid." *Charlotte.* He knew her damn name. It just came with too much emotion for him to say it.

"Okay," Morgan said.

The little one was limp, and her sweaty curls clung to her mother's neck.

"Is she sick?" he asked.

"Ear infection."

He reached out and grazed his fingertips down Charlotte's back. She looked miserable. "Is there anything I can do?"

Morgan wrinkled her nose. "No, I can handle it."

"I didn't say you couldn't. I'm offering my help. She's my daughter, too, you know." It felt good to finally assert it.

"Believe me, I know." She closed her eyes briefly, and when she opened them there was less tension on her face. "If you're serious about helping, I could use someone to run into town for some medicine. Kory Flemming was here, and she left a prescription, but Aunt Phyllis is in bed, and I'm dreading dragging Charlotte out like this."

"Done." This was perfect—a way to help out his kid while he kept his distance from her mother.

"Oh my God," Morgan breathed. "I really didn't expect you to agree. Thank you. Thank you so much!"

His pulse quickened. How sad was that? After she'd walked away and kept his kid from him, he still got a rush from something as simple as a little appreciation. *Reflex*, he thought. Old habits died hard and all that crap. But he wouldn't be pulled down that destructive road again. "Does she need anything else?"

Morgan touched the script to his hand. "Maybe some electrolyte drink. Ask the pharmacist. He can show you what it is. Wait, and let me give you money."

He balked. How much child support had he been deprived of paying in the last two years? "No. I owe her this … and a hell of a lot more."

Morgan stared at him again. "Thank you."

"You said that already." At least this time his heart rate didn't flinch.

Fifteen minutes later, Charlie walked into the pharmacy. Maybe he should've anticipated the way the pharmacist scrutinized the prescription. When the town's once-notorious addict rolled into the pharmacy, surely someone would think he was looking for narcotics. But he wasn't, and that wasn't even the biggest surprise. Nope. Fred Farr had to be floored by the last name on the prescription.

"Is there a problem?" Charlie asked.

Fred shook his head. "No. Absolutely not. I just … you have … have you …I mean, has she had a prescription filled here before?"

"No, she hasn't."

"Yes, well. I need an address and date of birth in order to fill this."

Charlie stretched the kinks out of his neck and signed. Address was a problem. He knew Phyllis's street, but he didn't know her box number. Birthdate? He knew that one by heart. When the paternity papers had reached him, he'd stared at the April date until he couldn't see straight anymore. It'd nearly killed him to sign away his rights, but he'd hoped their baby would have a good life, a better one than they could offer.

Turns out he could've saved himself the heartache.

In the end, he gave his address as Charlotte's address, and then he wandered around the pharmacy waiting for the prescription to be filled. He carried a six-pack of pediatric electrolyte drink in the crook of his arm, hopeful the stuff would perk her up a bit. He couldn't get the pitiful sight of her, limp and sweaty, out of his mind. Maybe she needed tissues. He tucked a box of Kleenex under his other arm.

As he made his way back to the pick-up window, a king-sized KitKat bar caught his eye. Morgan loved those things. At least she had. He used to buy them by the dozen when she'd been home from college and stressed out by her overbearing, overly critical parents.

He grabbed a bar and studied the packaging. *Don't do it, man.* And yet he couldn't get past how beaten up she'd looked. Maybe this would give her a boost … so she could better take care of Charlotte.

When he returned to Phyllis's house, he didn't bother knocking. He didn't want to wake them if they were sleeping. Turning the knob, he pushed inside to find Morgan and Charlotte cuddling on the recliner chair.

Morgan smiled at him. He wished he could muster some of the anger he'd felt the other day.

"Thank you so much," she whispered.

His pulse accelerated. *Don't be stupid. Do not fall for her again.* Three years and a baby didn't change the fact she couldn't be trusted. "No problem."

Charlotte didn't lift her head off Morgan's shoulder, but she watched him from the corners of her eyes. He reached into the bag and pulled out the medicine. "This is for you. It's going to make you feel better."

She wrinkled her nose just like Alice would have.

Charlie grinned. "She doesn't like medicine?"

"Who does?"

He freed the six-pack of pink electrolyte drink from the bag. "How about this?"

She hid her face against Morgan's chest.

He shrugged and set the drink on the coffee table beside the medicine. "It looks like the man strikes out."

Morgan shook her head. "You get three strikes before you're out. You'll do better when she isn't sick."

Maybe he would. Maybe he wouldn't. There was a good chance he wasn't cut out for this fatherhood thing no matter how hard he tried. He hadn't had the best role model.

"Charlie, about the other day. I don't want bad blood between us. I really am sorry. I know they're just words, but I'm going to find a way to prove it to you—for our daughter's sake."

Our daughter's sake. They had a kid. Together. Holy shit. How surreal was that?

"What else is in the bag?" Morgan's eyes sparkled.

He'd forgotten about that. Could she see the orange packaging through the white plastic bag?

He pulled his hands behind his back. Another reflex. It seemed eerily natural to tease her.

"Charlie … " she grinned, "what's in the bag?"

Years ago, she would've teased him, too. She would've backed him into a corner and searched every ounce of his body until she found the chocolate. His muscles tightened on the memory.

He dropped the bag into her lap. "It's no big deal. You just looked like you were having a bad day."

She stared at him. "Try a bad year."

Aside from her parents turning to a life of crime, whose fault was that exactly? His jaw ticked. So much for keeping a lid on the anger. "I wanted to be there for you."

Her eyes rolled upward, and he could see the tears on her lashes. "I know you did. I made a mistake." She gave a half-laugh. "I've made a lot of mistakes. And I'm so sorry about most of them. But I'm not sorry about her. Please, don't let how you feel about me get in the way of how you feel about her. You're more than welcome to hate me."

He looked at the bag in her lap and then the child in her arms. It was too late for that, wasn't it? The best he could do was to keep her at a distance.

Maybe then he wouldn't end up loving her again.

Chapter Five

"You are still one popular girl." Aunt Phyllis let the curtain fall back into place. "That 'Mama's Boy' Mitchell is here to see you."

"Mark?" Morgan gave Charlotte the building block she'd been holding and stood. "Why would Mark come see me?"

"Well, he sure as heck isn't here to see me. Answer the door and find out. I'll sit with baby girl." Aunt Phyllis made a silly face at Charlotte, who laughed.

Thank God she was feeling better. Twenty-four hours after starting the antibiotic, and she was like a different kid.

Morgan was feeling remarkably good, too. Good enough to smile when she answered the door.

"Hey," Mark said. He looked nervous, shifting his weight from one foot to the other, flashing his eyes all over the place. "I just dropped my mother off at ladies' bible study, and I had some time to kill. How's the little one?"

"Good. Better. Thank you so much for coordinating things with Kory."

He smiled.

It felt weird to have someone checking in on her, especially a Mitchell.

"Invite the boy in," Aunt Phyllis said.

Morgan nodded. "I was about to. Mark, would you like to come in and meet my little girl."

"Sure."

Charlotte sat on the couch next to her aunt, who held a kitten in her lap.

"You know my Aunt Phyllis, don't you?"

"I do." Mark reached forward for a handshake. "Nice to see you again."

God only knew the last time he'd seen her. Aunt Phyllis was patently against going into town except for emergencies. That's what had made her offer to run to the pharmacy so thoughtful.

"And this is my Charlotte. Baby, this is Mommy's friend. His name is Mark. Can you say 'hi'?"

She opened her mouth like she was going to say "hello," but then a cat that had leapt onto the window ledge distracted her. "See dat cat?"

"She's sweet," Mark said.

"She is."

"She looks … " But he stopped cold.

Like Alice Cramer. It was so true Morgan couldn't even flinch. She used to think Charlotte's physical similarities to Charlie's sister were karmic payback, too. But the more she fell in love with Charlotte, the less she cared. She didn't even see the resemblance anymore—unless someone pointed it out.

"Time to feed the chickens," Aunt Phyllis announced.

Charlotte scurried off the couch. "Me feed."

"Ask Mommy first."

"Me feed," Charlotte said again, this time facing Morgan.

How could she say no to that face? The teen years were going to be hell. "Okay, but be careful. Keep her high enough that she doesn't get pecked."

After the screen door banged, Morgan waved Mark into the kitchen, where they could continue their talk while she kept one eye trained out the window over the sink.

"How's the job hunt coming?"

"It stalled with Charlotte being ill." Having a sickly kid was an employment curse.

"Have you given anymore thought about working at Charlie's?"

Putting herself in close proximity to Charlie on a regular basis wasn't a good idea. Not after last night. She'd expected a colossal confrontation when he'd showed up again. She hadn't expected him to offer his help, and then bring her back a candy bar. She smiled faintly as she thought about the half a KitKat tucked behind the milk in the fridge.

But that little spark between them didn't erase the anger and mistrust she suspected Charlie was struggling with. "Charlie wouldn't want me working there."

About thirty yards from the house, Aunt Phyllis sat Charlotte on an inoperable riding lawn mower and filled her hand with chicken feed.

"Are you sure about that?" Mark asked. "Rumor has it Charlie was trolling around Farr's Pharmacy with a six-pack of pediatric electrolyte drink in his hands."

It was such silly gossip, Morgan should've laughed. But she chewed the inside of her cheek instead. Being the target of Morgan-related town gossip would only piss him off more. "Charlie was helping me out. He went into town and got Charlotte's prescription filled."

"And you don't think he'd help you out again by letting you work at the bistro?"

She shot him a mind-your-own-business look.

"What? I'm trying to help."

"*Why* are you trying to help? And don't give me crap about rooting for the outcasts."

"Honestly?" He strummed his fingers on the table. "I'm afraid that restaurant is going to close unless something drastic happens. It's plagued by rumors of poor service and Charlie's strict adherence to his menus. He wields that no substitutions rule like it's 'off with their heads.'" He laughed, but then he grew serious.

"And you think me working there is going to turn things around? I don't see how. If people are staying away now, they'll only come around to burn the place down once they hear I'm there."

He grinned. "I'm surprised you and Alice never got along. You're just as melodramatic."

Morgan rolled her eyes, and then looked out the window in time to see Charlotte launching chicken feed into the air.

"I have a friend who works at the bistro. His name is Corbin. He was hired as the sous chef, but Charlie has had him waiting tables since the second or third week. He says Charlie's not a bad guy—just a little stressed out and misunderstood. You can relate to that, can't you?"

Morgan glared at him. "You are pushy, Mark Mitchell."

"Yep. I just want you to stop by the bistro and check it out. Maybe once you're there you'll see something you can do. It would benefit Charlotte to have her parents working together to make that place a success. Of course, it would benefit me, too. I don't often get to be the savior of things on the business end. If this works, and I convinced you to give it a try, then I'll have something to brag about at board meetings."

"You Mitchells. Always conniving in the name of your almighty family business."

"Guilty." He grinned.

She didn't need to be a pawn in another Mitchell game, but for some strange reason Mark had been incredibly nice to her and helped her when no one else would. "Fine. I'll visit the bistro, but I'm not making any promises. I still don't think he'll want me there."

It was going to take more than a KitKat bar to fix things between her and Charlie.

• • •

"I can't do this." Charlie's hostess-turned-waitress tossed her apron on the stainless steel prep counter and swatted at the tears running down her face.

"You can't do what?"

"Work here anymore."

"You're quitting in the middle of dinner service? Are you kidding me?" Charlie abandoned the plate of sea bass he'd been garnishing.

"No," Hannah yelled.

He threw up his hands. "You're yelling at me. Why are you yelling at me? I didn't yell at you once." He'd been biting his tongue ever since the call from Will.

"You didn't yell at me, but tables five and nine did. I told them the chef didn't allow substitutions or salt shakers. Five called me ridiculous, and then Nine walked out—just like I'm about to do." She stomped to the far side of the room and disappeared behind a partition that separated a tiny bank of lockers from the main kitchen space.

"Chef, I need that sea bass." Corbin, the skinny guy from Rileyville, who was supposed to be the sous chef, stood two steps inside the kitchen. Charlie couldn't believe the kid was still hanging around. He'd have bolted by now if someone had told him he had to wait tables. But this kid took food service serious, and he was the best waitperson Charlie had.

"Sea bass? You need sea bass? Well, I need another waitress," Charlie yelled, hoping Hannah would hear him. He tossed a garnish of chervil leaves on top of the fish and shoved the plate toward Corbin.

"I'm doing the best I can." The kid picked up the food and left in a huff.

Crap. That was all Charlie needed—for Corbin to quit, too.

"Hannah," Charlie called out, hoping he could convince his latest dissenter to stay at least through her current shift.

The slamming of the heavy metal door that led to the alley was his answer.

"Fuck!" With his hand strangling the stem of a meat mallet, he pounded the hell out of a chicken breast.

A few minutes later, the door creaked open again. Maybe she'd reconsidered. He exhaled. *Be nice. Beg if you have to.*

He glanced at the massive script tattoo running from his wrist to the inside of his elbow. *Think before you…*

Talk. He nodded. Tonight was definitely a *think before you talk* kind of night. He'd purposefully left the sentiment open-ended, so he could take from it whatever inspiration he needed. *Think before you talk. Think before you drink. Think before you act.* He probably should've shortened it to *think.* That seemed to be the key.

"Hey," said an unexpected, shaky voice that lifted Charlie's head as if his chin were caught on a fishing hook.

What the hell was Morgan doing in his kitchen?

Think before you talk.

"Is this a bad time? It is. I'm sorry. I should've called first." She stood before him wringing her hands, wearing a white blouse and black slacks that hugged her surprisingly curvy body.

A heavy warmth formed in his gut. Charlie would've laughed if he weren't trying so damn hard to think of words that wouldn't get him into bigger trouble than he was already in. This was ridiculous.

She pointed behind her. "I came through the back door, because I didn't want to cause a scene up front."

"Chef, table five is asking for their waitress."

"Their waitress quit." Charlie managed the words without adding the deep, angry growl rumbling around in his chest.

"You mean I'm the only one handling the dining room?"

"Unless you have some imaginary friends, then yes."

Corbin's jaw dropped. "I can't seat people, take orders, deliver meals, and bus tables all by myself."

"I can help," Morgan said.

He did not need her—and those curves—causing trouble around here. "No. This is not your job."

"It sort of is. Margaret offered to hire me."

He groaned. "Well, I'm un-offering. Go home to Charlotte."

Her brows furrowed. "I don't really have a home, Charlie. I need money to get a home, and I need a job to get money."

He reached to the pot rack overhead and ripped down a skillet. If the money he had wasn't already tied up as an investment in this restaurant and the renovation of his house, he'd have paid her every last drop of back child support she deserved just to get her out from under his skin.

Corbin walked into the room with his hands raised. "I don't want to get in the middle of whatever is going on in here, but we have a situation out there. People need food. Can we do that and handle this later?"

"Where do I get one of those notepads?" Morgan asked, pointing at Corbin.

"No," Charlie said again, but nobody was listening to him.

Corbin dug into the basket beside the door and tossed Morgan a tablet. "The menu changes weekly, so a mini-copy is taped to the notebook's cover. For God's sake, remember: absolutely no substitutions. Other than that we're BYOB. Most people bring a bottle of wine. You just open it and pour. Take the five tables to the left of the main aisle—only two are full right now. I'll take the rest."

And then they were gone, like a bad nightmare, leaving Charlie rattled and unable to find the "center" his sponsor talked so fondly about.

Deep breaths, Charlie thought as he dressed the chicken. He needed this restaurant to work if he ever hoped to prove he was more than a chip off Johnny Cramer's block—a guy who was a liability to this town and his family instead of an asset. He wanted to be the kind of man a child could look up to. And he needed to be able to face Morgan without falling apart if he ever wanted that child to be a regular part of his life.

But if she thought this was going to be easy, she was crazier than he was. And he was the least of her worries.

The people out there had chased sweet, little Hannah away. They wouldn't hesitate to do the same to Morgan.

• • •

One fast glance around the dining room told Morgan nobody particularly intimidating was here. Still, she'd thought the same thing while inside the credit union and the mini-mart, too.

Her hands shook. *You can do this.* It was waiting tables. How hard could it be?

"Good evening. My name is … " Her throat made a clicking sound when she swallowed. "My name is Morgan how can I help you? Can I start you off with something to drink?" She spoke fast and ran the words together hoping her name would get lost in the jumble.

"Morgan?" The sort-of-familiar-looking woman batted her lashes double time.

"That's my name." There was no use in denying it.

"You don't recognize me, do you?" The woman patted the skin framed by her V-neck sweater. "Jessica Plant. I played trumpet at your wedding. Well … I suppose I can still call it that. We did get to play the wedding march before Alice Cramer stood up and stopped the rest of the ceremony."

Okay, this was bad, but it wasn't horrible. Jessica wasn't being mean. "I do remember you. It's … nice to see you again." She smiled but diverted her eyes to the notepad. "Now, what can I get you to drink?" The less small talk the better.

Jessica handed over a bottle of wine for Morgan to cork and pour. And just like that, service for table seven was underway.

That went better than expected.

With her shoulders a little stronger and her back a little straighter, she made it to the kitchen, where Charlie was clutching a stainless steel bowl. One arm manned a whisk. The rapid whirling motion drew her attention straight to his tattooed forearm.

Her face heated. There was something about a man who knew his way around a kitchen. "Where would I find a corkscrew?" Her last word taunted her until the heat from her face nosedived straight into the depths of her belly.

He glanced up and his wrist slowed. When he shook his head, it was clear he still didn't want her here. "In the drawer beneath the glass rack. Keep one in your apron."

"Okay. Thanks for the tip."

The whisking resumed—only double time. He might not want her here, but he needed her here. They needed each other. Boy, was that a loaded thought.

Rushing out of the kitchen with corkscrew in hand, she found two more tables in her section were filled. A total of eight people needed service. Out of the eight, she recognized four. No one too scary.

She fumbled her way through the Plants' food orders, gathered fountain drinks for table nine, and introduced herself to table six.

"You're Robert Parrish's daughter, aren't you?" asked a man she didn't recognize.

Questions like that illustrated why she needed to get out of town before Charlotte was penalized for her last name. "I am."

"I hope he rots in jail."

"Peter!" The man's dinner date reached across the table and grabbed his wrist.

"No, I mean it. That bastard fixed bids and cost me a small fortune in lost jobs."

"I'm sorry," Morgan said. "He let a lot of people down." His daughter included.

"Your appetizers are up." Corbin touched a hand to her back as he passed. That little bit of warmth bolstered her.

When she returned to the kitchen, Charlie's back was to her. A plate of flash fried escarole and a hummus platter waited on the counter. She grabbed them both without saying anything. Silence was better than angry words.

Back into the fire she went. By now, lots of people were looking at her, but she couldn't care. She owed Charlie the helping hand. Besides, she finally had a job and a way out of Harmony Falls. She could handle this knowing it was only temporary.

Morgan set the appetizers on the Plants' table. "Here you go."

"What is this?" Jessica pointed to the pile of greens kissed with a crunchy coating.

"Flash-fried escarole." Morgan glanced at the flap of her notepad to double-check.

"I wanted escargot."

"Oh." She looked at the notepad again. "I don't believe we have escargot. Did your menu say escargot?"

"*You* said escargot was the special."

"Escarole. They're similar sounding but very different things."

Jessica's eyes narrowed. "Don't patronize me."

"I'm not. I'm trying to explain."

"Can I help over here?" Again, Corbin touched Morgan's back.

"She said escargot was on special, but she brought us a pile of weeds instead."

Corbin picked up the plate. "I apologize for the mistake. Unfortunately, we don't have escargot. How about I take this off your bill and comp you a free appetizer and desserts instead? Charlie Cramer makes the best chocolate cake around."

"I really am sorry about that." Morgan forced a smile. What she really wanted to do was scream, *I said escarole. It's not my fault you heard escargot.* Escargot. In a Harmony Falls bistro. Who did these people think they were? But, at least one good thing came from being raised by image-obsessed parents—Morgan knew when to bite her tongue. She knew how to play the game, and she wasn't about to make Charlie resent having her here any more than he already did.

"If you want, I'll switch tables with you." Corbin fell in step with her as they walked away. "Table two. They're my parents. They'll be nice and easy."

They were.

And when the last customer finally left the building, Morgan was convinced that, after a good night's sleep, she'd be ready to do this all over again.

Chapter Six

Charlie's office phone rang as he cleaned up the kitchen. He glanced at the wall clock. *After ten.* Who was calling here? Probably a wrong number. He could always check Caller ID. Or, he could ignore it.

He wiped the prep space until it shined. Once Morgan and Corbin finished in the dining room, Charlie was going to thank her for her help, pay her in cash out of the register drawer, and tell her she didn't need to return.

Every time she walked into the kitchen, the air thinned. Every time she smiled, he blanked. And that couldn't happen. He needed to keep his mind clear around her—otherwise he'd end up burned again.

The restaurant needed help, but it couldn't come from her. No, he needed someone he could trust to stick by him. He was done with people who ran away.

The phone rang again.

Somebody wanted to get a hold of him. He walked into his office on the third ring, and saw *Unknown Caller* on the display. If it was a wrong number, he could just hang up. "Hello."

"Charlie."

Will. Charlie squeezed his eyes shut and covered his face with his free hand.

"Guess where Kory and I had dinner tonight?"

He was not in the mood for guessing games. "I don't know. Where?"

"At the Caldreas's house. You can imagine our surprise when Hannah came home crying and saying she quit her job at the bistro because she didn't want to be a waitress."

"I didn't yell at her. You told me to be nice, and I was nice." He'd barely spoken to her all evening to make sure.

"I don't know what happened, Charlie, and I don't care. You have one person helping you now—Corbin. I'm starting to agree with my mother; rescinding our financial support and putting that money into a bakery would be much less hassle."

Charlie sniffed. Without the Mitchells' help, he'd be as good as closed.

Voices sounded in the kitchen. *Corbin and Morgan.* Wait! Technically, he had more than one person helping him. It wasn't perfect, but if it saved his ass … "I already have a replacement for Hannah."

"You hired someone else on your own?"

"No, your mother did. Morgan Parrish."

Silence.

Charlie sunk into his desk chair. Good God, things had just gone from bad to crazy. Now, he was going to have to work with Morgan until they found her replacement.

"Wow," Will said. "I did not see that coming. What the hell was my mother thinking?"

"Beats the hell out of me."

"Is she any good?"

"She managed. End of the night, and she's still here."

"Hey, that's more than we can say for most of them."

Charlie dropped his head to the desk. She was still more than capable of walking out on him tomorrow or the next night. Maybe he should take bets on when.

"Okay. Then I'll try to get Hannah back to hostessing since Morgan's going to waitress," Will said.

At least something good should come of this.

When he'd hung up the phone, he buried his face in his hands. If he weren't sober, he'd be drunk by now. He opened the bottom desk drawer and grabbed a bottle of spring water. He polished it off in five seconds flat.

"Night." Morgan stood in the doorway. She tipped her head and settled her gaze on the bottle in his hands.

"Water." His defensive streak was still so strong.

"I know." She smiled softly. "Thanks for giving me this chance."

He nodded and tossed the empty bottle into the trash. He didn't want to give her any chances to let him down again, but he needed her—temporarily—or he was going to run this place into the ground. He couldn't afford to go it alone just yet.

"If you want, you're welcome to stop by and see Charlotte tomorrow. She's feeling much better now." She tipped her head to the other side. "Thanks again for everything you did that night."

Did it make him a bad man to wish he hadn't done a damn thing? Then, maybe she wouldn't be staring at him like there weren't miles of stagnant water between them.

He grunted like none of it mattered. Maybe that made him a jerk, but if he had to work with Morgan every night except Sunday and Monday, he had to maintain some emotional distance. And he wasn't sure about seeing Charlotte tomorrow, either.

Self-preservation was the name of the game. He had to put himself first. After everything she'd done, he couldn't trust Morgan to do that.

• • •

"Morgan Parrish, is that you?"

Three tables into her second night waitressing at Char-Grilled Bistro, Morgan hated that question enough to dream about quitting.

"Yes, it is," she said, smiling at the woman who looked familiar, but not familiar enough to prompt a name.

"You've gained weight," the woman said. "Don't you think?" she asked the man across the table from her.

The man offered Morgan a weak smile. "I don't notice those things."

"Oh, sure you do. Morgan Parrish used to look like a supermodel. Men notice *those* things."

She wanted to crawl in a hole, but there were no tips in a hole, and she needed tips to make this nightmare worthwhile.

Miraculously, the couple managed to order without any more insults, and Morgan moved on to fill the water glasses at table eight.

Bruce Carter, the local logging baron, lifted a stainless steel cup of whipped butter from the bread basket. "This is real butter. Could I get some margarine? I've got to take care of the ticker."

"Of course."

Instead of a "thank you" when Morgan filled her water glass, Karena Carter offered the same patronizing sneer she'd been wearing since she sat down.

What was the advice Corbin had given her last night while they'd been cleaning up? *You're here temporarily. They're mean permanently. Pity them, not the other way around.* Yeah, that.

When she reached the kitchen, Charlie stood with his back to the door, shaking a frying pan over the stove. Dressed in a white t-shirt and jeans with his tattoos on display and a skullcap covering his head, he looked more like a renegade biker than a chef. She'd always been drawn to that lack of propriety. *Yum.* What was it about those bad guys?

But Charlie wasn't a bad guy—even though he'd been giving her some serious cold shoulder. No, he was a good guy, who ran to the pharmacy for a child he'd just met, and while he'd been there, he'd purchased a KitKat bar for a woman who'd lied to him. And now, he'd acquiesced to giving that woman a job, under his feet.

Hell, he wasn't just a good guy; he was a saint.

He reached above him for a bowl, and his bicep flexed.

She pressed a hand to her chest, because saints didn't look like that. And then she stuck her head in one side of the mammoth refrigerator, hoping to cool herself down.

"What are you doing?"

"Table eight wants margarine."

"I don't have margarine."

She glanced at him. He was hunched over lamb chops like a culinary mad scientist. "Really? Well, you should have margarine for people who are worried about their arteries."

"No, I shouldn't. Margarine is one fucking molecule away from crude oil. How's that good for anyone's arteries?"

Was he serious? She shut the fridge and stared at him. "You don't have to eat it or cook with it, but it would be nice to have it for people who do."

He glared at her. "Don't tell me how to run my kitchen. Get your ass back out there and tell table eight we don't do margarine here."

Her jaw dropped. Was this display just for her, or was this the man who'd been chasing everyone away? "Charlie, I know you're mad at me, and on some level I deserve the attitude, but please tell me you don't talk to other people like that."

"If you don't like it, sweetheart, then leave."

Eww. Her father had been patronizing, too. "I'd love to leave. I really would, but that wouldn't do either of us any good. You'd be down one waitress, and I'd be struggling to find a way out of this God forsaken town … again."

Charlie frowned. "I just want to be left alone so I can cook."

"Then cook at home, Charlie, because cooking here means you have to learn to compromise or you're not going to be cooking here long."

He turned his back on her.

So much for sainthood. She glanced at the clock on the wall above the door as she left the kitchen. Four more hours and she was out of here—at least for tonight.

After she told Bruce Carter they were out of margarine, she delivered table seven's orders, and then cleared table nine. Not until she reached the register, which was separated from the main dining room by a burlap curtain, did she realize Jack Kelley hadn't included a tip. In the space where numbers representing the customary fifteen percent of the bill should've been was the message: *Get your tip from your father, since he robbed me blind.*

She crinkled the receipt and drilled it into the garbage can. How could her father have robbed the town sheriff blind? It would've been one ballsy move. Then again, her father was a narcissist being held without bail in a federal prison. That pretty much indicated he was capable of anything.

She retrieved the receipt, smoothed it out, and slipped it into the register. As much as she wanted to erase the words, she couldn't screw Charlie out of the income.

"Can I get in here?" Corbin pressed behind her.

"Yep." She stepped aside and saw him smile.

"Table eight's meals are up."

He was such a sweet guy. At least somebody around here with a penis was.

Back in the kitchen, Morgan grabbed table eight's plates from the edge of the stainless steel counter. Charlie glanced up from the pasta he was tossing. Their eyes met for a second, but that was it.

Four more hours—less than, she reminded herself, trying not to be discouraged by the fact that tomorrow she had to do it all over again. It would get easier. There would be good nights and bad nights. Eventually, she wouldn't need this paycheck, and Charlie wouldn't need her help. They'd be even then.

When she stepped into the dining room, Bruce and Karena Carter were waiting for their sea bass. She could handle them—including Karena's bitchy smile. She'd get over Jack Kelley not tipping her, too. But seeing Hannah seat Justin and Alice at table nine just about did her in.

Morgan pawed at the collar of her blouse. Corbin needed to trade tables with her again, because there was no way she could wait on Justin and Alice.

Chin up. Shoulders back. Deliver the Carters' sea bass, and then pull Corbin aside.

But her brain didn't quite get the memo. When her upper body moved, her legs dragged, and the toe of her sensible black flats caught on the unvarnished oak planks.

Thud. Two pieces of sea bass slid off the plates and splattered on the floor.

Sound ceased. Time froze. She peeled the food off the floor and stumbled to the kitchen.

Charlie was waiting for her at the door. "What the hell happened?"

"I need two more sea bass." She shoved past him and locked herself in the bathroom.

• • •

Charlie knew exactly what had happened the minute he saw Alice and Justin at table nine. This night just kept getting better.

"I can handle it, Chef," Corbin said.

But Charlie waved him off.

Hannah stood at the hostess podium looking like she was ready to bolt again.

He needed a waitress more than he needed his sister's patronage. What the hell was she thinking coming in here?

You can't talk to people like that. Morgan's words from earlier rattled around in his brain.

So maybe asking Alice what the hell she was thinking wasn't the smartest thing to do. Instead, he would casually walk up and warn her to treat wait staff—all of them—with respect or leave.

Alice's eyes were wide and blazing blue. "What is *she* doing here?"

"Working." He lowered his voice, hoping she would follow his lead. "I figured you would've heard already."

"No, I hadn't heard." She glared at Justin.

He held up both hands. "I had no idea, either."

"She has to go, Charlie." Alice's voice rose. "This is a recipe for disaster."

Charlie shushed her. It was better than telling her to calm the hell down. "Please … " he gritted his teeth, "lower your voice. You're upsetting my staff and customers."

She rolled her eyes. "Oh, for crying out loud. When have you ever worried about something like that? You shouldn't be worried about me and my mouth. You should be worried about that lying, cheating woman in your kitchen. Why in the world did you hire her?"

"I didn't." He flashed a shitty grin at Justin. "Margaret did."

Alice took a noisy breath through her open mouth. "That is ridiculous. Justin, you need to talk to your mother right now. Or I will." She was shouting.

Charlie hit a fist on the table, and the silverware clanged. "Enough. I want you to leave. I can't afford to lose any more waitresses—or sea bass."

"You have got to be kidding."

Justin stood, holding a hand open to Alice. "Let's go. I've suddenly lost my appetite."

"This is not okay." She said it again as Justin led her out the door.

No, it wasn't okay, but it was his reality. He had to deal with it somehow.

He waited until they were on the sidewalk before he turned and asked the table beside him, "How's your meal?"

The couple just gaped at him, but the group at the next table raved about his tomato saffron broth and grilled polenta fries. That was good. He rubbed a crick from his neck as the compliments soaked in. Thank God, somebody was happy.

Corbin looked oddly happy, too. "I stirred the sauce, so the bottom didn't burn."

The kid was thrilled to be in the kitchen. If things ever calmed down around here *maybe* Charlie would loosen the reins. He nodded his thanks. "Is she still in the bathroom?"

"Yep."

"See if you can coax her out." He didn't want to get dragged into a conversation about what he'd done and why he'd done it.

With no time to spare, he got back to work, preparing the "make up" dishes. But he didn't stay locked in the kitchen. He found himself wandering in and out of the dining room when there was a lull in cooking, asking diners about their meals. If he kept a higher profile, people might focus more on him and the food and back off his wait staff.

Bruce Carter flagged him over. "Charlie, your polenta is better than my mother's, but don't you dare tell her I said that." The man had a genuine laugh, but his wife was distracted.

Charlie followed her cold stare to Morgan.

"How is *your* meal, Mrs. Carter?"

"Good now that it's here." She turned up her nose. "The service, on the other hand, is terribly lacking."

Charlie puffed out his chest. At least she was complaining to him and not Morgan or Corbin. He could take it without walking out. "We're just working out the kinks. Hopefully, you'll cut us some slack. Otherwise, you can stay home and serve yourself something barely edible." Charlie patted Bruce on the shoulder. "Thanks again for coming in."

He had a feeling that fell into the category of *you can't talk like that to people*, but he didn't give a rat's ass.

As he passed Morgan, who was balancing three plates, he noticed her biting the hell out of her bottom lip. He refused to acknowledge the hiccup in his heartbeat, but he did stop in the doorway to the kitchen and turn around to make sure she made it without dropping anything.

Of course, he was just worried about his sea bass.

After she settled the plates, she smiled at a child, whose parents he didn't recognize. The little girl lifted a polenta fry off her plate and raised it near Morgan's mouth. Despite the animated conversation she seemed to be having with the adults she was serving, she bent closer to the little girl and pretended to gobble the fry. The child cackled and Charlie felt a sharp pang.

He needed to see *his* little girl.

• • •

Morgan grabbed the opposite end of the table and lifted. With Corbin's help, the dining room was returned to its pristine, pre-dinner condition, and her mood was better than she expected it to be—especially after spilling the sea bass and hearing that Charlie had kicked Justin and Alice out.

When they'd tallied the receipts and closed up the register, Corbin slid a short stack of bills topped with some change toward her.

"What's this?" she asked.

"Tips. I'm splitting mine with you, because I noticed you didn't get your fair share. People are mean, and we peons need to stick together."

Morgan shook her head. "I can't take that. I didn't earn it."

"You earned twice this when you dropped the sea bass. It was like slapstick dinner theater." He laughed. "I'm sorry. Is it too soon?"

Morgan chuckled. "No, you're good. Thank you." She pushed the money toward him. "I never would've survived these last two nights without you."

"Tomorrow will be better."

"I hope so."

"I know so." He pushed the money toward her again. "I'll be here to make sure of it, unless my ship comes in and it's towing my very own bistro behind it. Then, you're on your own."

"Why don't you tell Charlie you want to cook more?"

"Because … " his voice grew louder at the end until he was almost shouting, "Charlie's a bastard, who chases everyone away, and *somebody* has to wait tables."

Charlie appeared in the doorway, wearing a half-smile. "If that's true, then why are you still here?"

Corbin rolled his eyes. "I'm here, because you'd be lost without me, silly. I'm the glue to this joint."

Charlie shot a dishtowel slingshot style at Corbin. "You're delusional."

Corbin laughed as he bent to retrieve the towel, leaving Morgan smiling at Charlie. He didn't drop the expression or look away. It was their first real connection all night.

The dishtowel hit Charlie square in the chest as Corbin waltzed by him and into the kitchen. "Whatever. See ya both tomorrow."

And then there were two. Morgan's palms grew clammy. Being completely alone with Charlie for the first time in three years was … unsettling.

She turned toward the counter and gathered up the money Corbin had left.

"I'd like to see Charlotte again."

She nodded and glanced at his reflection in the dining room window. "You were invited to come by earlier today. You didn't show."

"I know. I was … working through some things."

Like staying sober? God, she hoped not, but it was a real possibility. She wanted to believe his sobriety was unshakable, but his track record where she was concerned wasn't good. And if tonight proved anything it was that she wreaked havoc whenever she was around. He had to be stressed out by her return. Why wouldn't he be tempted to drink?

"Maybe I could come by tomorrow," he said.

Coordinating visitation hadn't been part of her plan when she'd headed to Harmony Falls from Connecticut. Her plan had been easy. Get the money, drop the bomb, and go—because surely he wouldn't want anything to do with them. She still wasn't convinced he knew what he wanted as far as Charlotte was concerned.

"She deserves more than maybes, Charlie. You have to be sure you want to be a part of her life even after we leave Harmony Falls. Phone calls, birthday cards, emails. If you're not sure you can handle that, then don't do this. She's young enough to forget."

His face contorted, and she felt horrible for saying it. "But if you are sure, then why don't you come to dinner on Sunday when the restaurant is closed?"

She didn't think it possible, but his face twisted even more.

"I'll think about it," he said.

Hopefully a stiff drink wasn't needed to help him make up his mind.

Chapter Seven

"Fish sticks go with macaroni and cheese," Aunt Phyllis sat crossed legged on the kitchen floor hand feeding a cat.

"I'm not going to serve a chef frozen fish sticks. It's bad enough I'm making him mac and cheese, but at least this is homemade."

"I thought he was coming to spend time with Charlotte."

"He is."

"Then why are you trying to impress him?"

Morgan set the slotted spoon on top of a folded paper towel and faced Aunt Phyllis. "I am not trying to impress him. Believe me, after everything I've done, there aren't enough tricks in the book to make Charlie see me as anything other than the woman who drove him to drink."

"Well, that's a shame. Charlie Cramer is a good catch."

Morgan laughed as she stirred the macaroni again, mostly because not too long ago she was considered "the catch," while her parents raged on about Charlie being the wrong man. "What do you know about good catches?"

Aunt Phyllis lifted the cat and cuddled it against her cheek. "I suppose not enough to catch one for myself."

Morgan's stomach turned. What a careless thing to say to a woman who'd spent her adult life alone. Hadn't she just lectured Charlie about the way he talked to people? "I'm sorry. I didn't mean it like that."

"Sure you did." She stood. "It's no secret I'm a loner, but I haven't always been, and I like having you and baby girl here. I'm not a complete kook."

"Of course you're not."

Morgan wished she knew more about Aunt Phyllis's life. She'd never been afforded many opportunities to be around her … until she had nowhere else to turn. Well she could make up for lost time now.

"So, if you weren't always a loner, tell me about him. What was his name?"

The metal colander Aunt Phyllis had been holding clattered into the sink.

Charlotte leapt to her feet and threw her arms around Morgan's leg.

"He was nobody," Aunt Phyllis said, her head shaking wildly. "He ended up not being a very good man."

How sad! And then suddenly the sadness gave way to an eeriness that had Morgan's neck hairs standing on end. Why did she have the feeling she knew the man? Probably because it was Harmony Falls, and everyone knew everybody. She shook off the weirdness by lifting Charlotte into her arms. "So he wasn't a good catch, huh?"

"Not at all." Aunt Phyllis wiggled a clean wooden spoon at Charlotte's belly. "Now, a man in cowboy boots who knows his way around a kitchen is a good catch, and don't you forget it."

Morgan laughed, but the tinny sound of the doorbell ringing had her clamming up fast. *Charlie.* There was still a part of her that expected him to bail at the last minute.

"I'll get it." Aunt Phyllis winked as she left the kitchen.

Morgan slicked a hand over her tied-back hair and smoothed her T-shirt, then kissed Charlotte's forehead. "Your daddy's here."

She headed to the living room with as much poise as she could muster.

Charlie stood beside Aunt Phyllis. A floppy teddy bear dangled from his right hand.

Sweet. She smiled. He was really going to make a go of this.

Charlotte buried her face in Morgan's neck.

"Hey," she said, trying her damnedest not to give into the urge to sneak a peek at those boots.

"Hey." He shoved his free hand into his pocket and smiled back.

"I'll go stir the macaroni," Aunt Phyllis said.

"Come on in."

She walked to the couch, and Charlotte's grip tightened.

"It's okay, Baby," she whispered in her ear.

And it would be okay, just not easy.

When she sat, Charlie sat, too.

"I brought her something better than medicine this time." He switched the bear to his other hand and rubbed his palm on his jeans.

The show of nervousness might have been even sweeter than the teddy bear.

"Charlotte, did you see this bear?" Morgan asked.

She shook her head.

"Well, look at it, silly." Morgan nudged her with a shoulder, hoping she would sit up and face him. "Charlie ... I mean ... your daddy brought it for you." Morgan's voice cracked when she made eye contact with Charlie, who looked like he was feeling equally unsure.

Maybe there was another way they should be handling this.

Charlotte shook her head again.

Charlie leaned forward, resting his elbows on his knees, dangling the stuffed animal in his hands, and then he looked back at them. "That's okay, kiddo. You came as a surprise to me, too. It's just going to take a while to get used to each other."

Morgan offered an encouraging smile as she turned Charlotte around in her arms to face Charlie. "You like teddy bears, don't you? Look at this one. He has a blue ribbon."

Morgan reached for the bear, brushing Charlie's hand with her fingertips. Heat pricked a path up her arm. It had been three years since she'd touched him. One little sweep shouldn't matter ... but it did. And that scared her. This wasn't a game. There was no room for any more mistakes. Charlotte's welfare came first.

Squeezing the bear harder than necessary, Morgan bounced the toy on Charlotte's thigh. "We can call him Mac for mac and cheese. How 'bout that?"

"Mac and cheese," Charlotte repeated, her little nose scrunching. She giggled when the bear's nose tickled the crook of her neck.

"Mac and cheese is Charlotte's favorite food." When Morgan looked up, Charlie's eyes were shiny. Tears. *Shoot.* Maybe the mistake had already been made. Maybe he wasn't ready for this. Maybe none of them were. She should have thought of that before she rushed into town.

She passed the bear to Charlotte, and swallowed her own surge of tears.

Oblivious to the heavy emotion, Charlotte bounced the bear off Morgan's face. "Mac eats you."

That brought the smile back to Charlie's face. "Hey, Charly," he said, smoothing his index finger down the inside of Charlotte's leg. "Do you like that bear? What's his name? Mac?"

Charly. Morgan hadn't had the guts to call Charlotte by that nickname, even though she knew somebody, sometime, would. It seemed perfectly appropriate for that somebody to be her father and namesake.

"Dinner is served," Aunt Phyllis called from the kitchen.

Charlie stood, and Morgan put Charlotte on the ground, taking her hand. "How 'bout you walk, and I'll carry the bear?" Maybe if *she* carried the bear, Charlotte would let Charlie hold her other hand.

Charlotte shook her head and tightened her grip on the stuffed animal. "No. My bear."

"At least she likes the bear," Charlie said.

"Baby steps." Morgan said. That was the only way they were going to get through this.

After Charlotte was settled in the booster seat, Morgan looked at the table Aunt Phyllis had set. A plate was missing. "We need one more."

Aunt Phyllis waved her off. "No, we don't. I'm not feeling well, so if you'd excuse me."

"Did you eat the macaroni and cheese?" Charlie eyed the steaming plate in front of him.

"Heavens no. I don't eat macaroni and cheese without fish sticks." She stared straight at Charlie's back, dropping her chin and bobbing her brows in the general direction of his boots.

Morgan turned her head to hide her shock. She hoped Charlie hadn't sensed Aunt Phyllis's obvious attempt to manipulate an innocent dinner into some kind of warped courtship.

Charlotte picked at her macaroni with both hands.

"Use your fork, honey." Morgan patted the neglected, plastic utensil.

Charlotte simply ignored it and shoved a handful into her mouth.

"What can I say? She's a little rough around the edges." It was something her mother had said the one and only time she'd visited her granddaughter. At the time, it had seemed like a direct dig at the child's Cramer lineage.

"There's nothing wrong with that," Charlie said.

When Morgan glanced at him, he was watching Charlotte shovel more into her mouth. He'd always had such a strong jawline and flawless lips.

She looked at her plate. "I know it's not gourmet, so I won't be offended if you don't eat it. But, I can promise you there's no margarine."

He chuckled, and she had no choice but to look at him again.

"What did you end up telling that guy?"

"That we were out of margarine."

"Much more diplomatic than I would've been. Ever since I stopped drinking, I've had a crazy short fuse." He slid a forkful of macaroni into his mouth. As he chewed, his brows rose. "This is good."

"You look surprised."

"I'm definitely surprised you cook anything."

"It's a newer skill cultivated from a lack of money and a little girl who loves pasta and cheese, but I'm a one-trick pony. Otherwise, it's PB&J and canned soup."

She helped Charlotte reach her sippy cup, and wiped a piece of macaroni from her chin. When she looked at Charlie again, he was studying her.

It was unnerving.

She focused on Charlotte again, and grabbed at the first innocuous thing that came to mind. "Let's show Daddy how smart you are. Where's your nose?"

Charlotte pointed to her nose, leaving a cheesy fingerprint in her wake.

"Good girl. Where's your chin?"

She smacked her fingertips below her mouth.

"Where's your mouth?"

She slapped her lips.

"Good girl! Where's your belly?"

Charlotte lifted her shirt and punctuated the action with a silly grin.

Charlie laughed. The lines deepened at the corners of his sparkling eyes. God, how long had it been since she'd seen him laugh?

He was so handsome.

Charlotte pointed at him. "Belly," she squealed as she patted her rounded stomach with her other hand.

Charlie wrinkled his nose. "You don't want to see my belly. It's hairy." He stuck out his tongue.

"Belly!" Charlotte shouted, rearing onto her knees and reaching across the small table to pinch Charlie's shirt.

He laughed again. "Boy, you're pushy … just like your mother." He grinned at Morgan before he turned his attention back to Charlotte again. "Fine. Belly." He lifted the edge of his T-shirt and gave the flat surface a smack.

Damn. She tore her gaze away from Charlie's abs and settled it on Charlotte, who was bouncing on her knees, giggling and smiling.

"Belly!" Charlotte screamed, and this time she reached for Morgan.

"No! You've seen mine lots of times." It wasn't nearly as impressive as Charlie's.

Morgan jumped up, grabbed her plate, and walked to the sink. This was not going to work. No more "family" dinners. Nothing good could come from repeated bonding like this. It would only make it harder on Charlie and Charlotte when Morgan had enough money to leave town.

She moistened a paper towel so she could clean Charlotte's face and hands. When she turned around, she saw Charlotte holding a mashed piece of macaroni inches from Charlie's mouth. He was probably going to nudge her hand away. It took one heck of a person to accept already-been-played-with food.

He wrinkled his nose, but he opened his mouth, and he smiled while he chewed.

Morgan faced the sink. Aunt Phyllis was right. Charlie Cramer was a good catch, but not because of his cooking skills or his cowboy boots—or even his flat stomach. Because surprisingly Charlie was a natural when it came to being a dad.

"Hey, sit," he said. "You cooked. I'll clean up."

A *good* catch? How about a *great* catch? But not for her. That line had snapped three years ago, and she would never use Charlotte as bait.

•••

Charlie sat on the floor beside the coffee table in Phyllis's living room, building a house with playing cards. He couldn't get the structure past two stories high without Charlotte knocking it down. But, he didn't care. When she giggled, microscopic fireworks exploded in his chest.

He hadn't expected to enjoy her this much.

"How do I go about paying child support? Is that something we can work out between us, or does the law need to get involved?"

"I don't want your money, Charlie."

"But you need my money. She needs my money."

Morgan nodded as she sat on the couch behind Charlotte, worrying her bottom lip. Her dark hair was pulled into a ponytail again. Come to think of it, he hadn't seen it down since she'd been back in Harmony Falls. He liked it this way. Low maintenance, without the ultra-shiny, inky strands competing for attention with her face. Her face with those piercing green eyes and strawberry lips had always been his downfall.

"We can work it out between us."

Charlotte dropped her diapered bottom into Charlie's lap as she took a card from his hand. She attempted to start the second story, but the cards crumbled, and she laughed. He liked how she found joy in what most people would consider to be failure. It gave him hope that she could grow up finding joy in him instead of resenting the mistakes he made.

Morgan moved from the couch to a spot on the floor near the toy basket, and Charlotte left his lap to cuddle up with her.

The child was asleep in minutes.

"She's my little narcoleptic," Morgan said. She smiled as she smoothed Charlotte's sunny hair.

They were like a beautiful, peaceful painting, but he recognized the trouble with seeing them that way. There'd been nothing peaceful about being with Morgan in the past. So what if she cooked, wore less makeup, and pulled her hair into a ponytail. Those were surface changes. He still couldn't trust her with his heart.

"I'm going to go," he said, standing and shaking his jeans over his boots. He hoped to shake off the layer of raw emotion that was weighing him down, too.

"Okay," Morgan whispered. "I'm so glad you came. It went well, didn't it?" A warm smile lit her face.

He nodded as he slid a crooked finger over Charlotte's rosy cheek. "Thanks for dinner." But he wasn't going to be making a habit of it.

Next time he'd ask to spend time with his daughter alone. It would be far less complicated.

Chapter Eight

"Could we give our compliments to the chef?" asked a friendly redhead as she exchanged conspiratorial glances with the brunette across the table and handed Morgan the billfold.

"Sure, I'll let him know you enjoyed your meals." Morgan snuck a peak at the credit card sticking out of the top. She didn't recognize the face or the last name, which meant this particular bill should be paid along with a tip.

"We were hoping to do it in person." The woman grinned. "We drove all the way from Puckett just to see him."

Morgan matched her grin when on the inside she felt a tightening. She didn't have a right to be jealous of any female attention Charlie received, but last night's dinner had made her feel a territoriality she had no business feeling. She hadn't come back to Harmony Falls to rekindle anything, and she sure as hell wasn't staying. "Red" on the other hand seemed harmless.

"Customer satisfaction is my top priority," Morgan said. "Let me see if he can spare a minute or two."

Charlie reluctantly agreed, but he smiled his way through whatever was happening at the table while Morgan and Corbin watched from behind the partition. Watching him with the clearly enamored women was eye-opening. Surely he'd had dates—even a girlfriend—over the past few years. Maybe he even had one now. He hadn't mentioned one, but it was possible.

"Do you think he'll ask the redhead out?" Morgan asked, trying to sound nonchalant.

"Maybe," Corbin said. "But I would be surprised."

"Why?"

"As far as I know, he's had his eye on someone else."

Morgan's heart flipped. "Who?"

"Carrie something. She's from around here and used to come in regularly."

Carrie was a common name, but for the life of Morgan, she couldn't remember a single one in Harmony Falls. "Why doesn't she come in anymore?"

"I don't know. I just haven't seen her in a while."

Probably since I got here. Shoot. He'd given her a job. He was paying child support. He was being nice to her. And her payback to him was screwing up his life again.

Morgan grabbed the water pitcher and walked to table seven, where Gertrude Cash and Tubby Stanwick, two of Alice's biggest fans, were making eyes at each other over their candied-walnut salmon. Refilling the glasses was part of her job, but she already knew this was one table that wouldn't yield a tip.

"Poor Alice," Gertrude said as she gave Morgan the stink-eye. "Knowing you're back in town and with her brother again has to be hard to swallow."

"There's nothing to swallow," Morgan said as pleasantly as possible. "Charlie and I aren't together, and I'm not staying in Harmony Falls."

The sneer slipped from Gertrude's lips. "You don't say."

"I do say." Morgan smiled, thankful something seemed to reduce the hostility. Maybe if she was more forthcoming with all her critics, it would have the same effect. "As soon as I find a new job and have enough money to relocate, I'm out of here."

Gertrude and Tubby gave her a five-dollar tip.

The theory held true the next day, too, when Wren Cannon, Alice's friend and assistant at the theater, brought her grandmother in for a birthday dinner and left a full twenty percent after hearing Morgan proclaim she wasn't interested in Charlie as anything more than a father to Charlotte.

It was a wonder what a little peace and money could do.

Morgan relaxed, letting the next few days unfold. She spent days with Charlotte and Aunt Phyllis and evenings at the restaurant cracking jokes with Corbin. It was a welcomed, monotonous rhythm after the upheaval of the last few months. She wasn't even rattled when Mrs. Mitchell and Mark appeared for their customary Friday evening reservation and insisted on sitting in her section.

"You should never fill a water glass that full," Margaret complained. "People with a weaker constitution might spill."

Mark laughed. "You do not have a weak constitution, Mother."

"But I will keep that in mind for other guests." Morgan hid a smile.

Later on in the evening, Mark stopped Morgan outside the kitchen. "Things look like they're going well."

"They're much better. I haven't spilled anything lately, and Charlie hasn't thrown anyone out, either. I'm sure you heard about what happened when your brother came in."

He nodded. "Something that juicy spreads like wildfire around Harmony Falls."

She bet it did. Morgan Parrish dumping two plates full of fish and running off to the ladies' room had to make half the population's day. "Thankfully the bistro is closed Sunday and Monday, which means I have two days off to hide up on the hill and lick my wounds before I have to face everyone again."

"I don't buy you're that wounded. Your constitution is about as weak as my mother's."

Morgan laughed.

"Table eight would like their waitress," Corbin said as he passed. He added a head nod and a blinding smile directed at Mark. "Good evening, Mr. Mitchell."

"Ooh, Mr. Mitchell," Morgan teased. "And here I thought Will and Justin had all the power."

It felt good to have someone to tease. When was the last time she had an honest-to-God friend?

Apparently, Mark felt the same, because he called on Sunday morning to say he had an unexpectedly free afternoon, and since she did too, she agreed to lunch in the park with him as long as Charlotte could tag along. But then Charlie called, asking if *he* could see Charlotte again, and an enormous part of Morgan—the part with the racing heart—wanted to cancel on Mark so she could spend the day with Charlie.

She didn't know what to do.

"I sort of have plans today," Morgan said as she paced the linoleum floor in the kitchen while Charlotte was out back with Aunt Phyllis feeding the chickens. "Would tomorrow work?"

"I can't do tomorrow. I have three windows being delivered, and I have to yank out the existing ones and install the new ones before it rains. But listen, does Charlotte have to go with you? Could she stay with me for a few hours?"

Crap. It was completely reasonable for a father to spend unsupervised time with his child. The courts would back Charlie up on that. Besides, Morgan had seen how good he was with Charlotte. And he was only going to get better. He was arguably more stable than a woman who harbored thirty-six cats and treated her small band of livestock with children's pain reliever.

"You can trust me," he added.

She thought about the liquor. He'd done lots of untrustworthy things while he was under the influence. Yet she couldn't imagine him putting Charlotte at risk. It was just motherhood making her overly paranoid, wasn't it?

"I don't know, Charlie."

"Then I'll stay at Phyllis's so we're in familiar territory and I have backup."

How could Morgan argue with that? But just to be sure she didn't wig out at the last minute and try to sabotage the daddy-daughter day, she left an hour before Charlie was supposed to arrive. As she drove to meet Mark at a picnic shelter on a blue-sky, Sunday afternoon, Morgan couldn't keep herself from wondering what Charlie and Charlotte would do for two hours. Aunt Phyllis had made homemade play dough. Charlotte liked to eat it. Charlie was going to have his hands full with that.

Two hours. She tightened her grip on the steering wheel. They'd be fine alone.

She'd be fine, too.

When Morgan pulled into the gravel parking lot, Mark was already there, standing alongside his shiny black sedan. She met him on the grass, suddenly conscious of how this might look. She'd messed things up with one Mitchell, and now she'd moved on to the only other eligible one. Then again, who was going to see them? Mark said this place would give Charlotte room to run and Morgan the best chance at a peaceful afternoon.

He gripped a grocery bag in each hand. "No Charlotte?"

She shook her head. "She's with Charlie."

"That's great. It looks like things are going well."

"They are. She's warming up to him, and he's good with her."

"And work is going smoothly?" He set the bags on the nearest picnic table.

"Surprisingly. I also managed to get to the library for some job searching, and I sent out some resumes."

"Excellent."

She helped him unload napkins, utensils, two foot-long hoagies, a tub of macaroni salad, a bag of potato chips, a box of lemonade drink pouches … and a six-pack of beer.

He wore a sheepish grin. "My mother doesn't like the smell of beer, so I sneak one when I'm going to be gone long enough for her not to notice."

Morgan laughed. "But you brought a six pack."

"It seemed silly and a little desperate to just bring one. Besides, I thought you might want to share." He cracked open a can and sipped. "Some days that just hits the spot."

Morgan pulled a lemonade pouch from the box in front of her. "Are you with your mother seven days a week?"

"Pretty much."

"That sounds rough."

"It is. She can be demanding."

"I understand. Charlotte can be demanding, too."

"Yeah, but Charlotte can't swear, yet, and she doesn't sign your paychecks, either. Plus, she's cute. That makes it more tolerable."

"And I have help." Aunt Phyllis was a godsend.

"How is living with Phyllis?" He slid half a turkey hoagie toward Morgan and opened the bag of chips.

"More normal than you might think. She's up at the crack of dawn and makes a hot breakfast every day, and she reads the bible before bed every night. In between, she gardens, bakes, cooks some more, and tends to her animals."

"No cat curled into a hat on her head and no gun by the door to shoot trespassers?"

Morgan smiled. "No."

"Why do you think she stays away from town?"

"For the same reason I'm eating lunch in a picnic pavilion instead of at the Main Street Diner. People suck. I'm sure she knows what they're saying about her. Trust me. Knowing people are talking about you behind your back is no fun—even if you deserve the chatter."

He faced the thick row of trees beyond the pavilion, as if the conversation had suddenly turned uncomfortable for him. Odd. Certainly she had more to be uncomfortable about as far as gossip went than he did. No matter what people thought about him hanging around his mother, he was still an almighty Mitchell.

"What do you think of my friend, Corbin?" He looked at her.

She lifted her brows at the abrupt change in topic. "I love Corbin. I think I would've quit by now if it weren't for him."

"Good." He grinned and slapped a spoonful of macaroni salad onto her paper plate. "Now, tell me about these jobs you applied for."

Another topic change. She would've called him on it if it weren't such a beautiful, peaceful day. Morgan sucked lemonade through the tiny drink pouch straw and glanced at the flock of birds squawking and flying in a V-shape over her head. Charlotte would like that. Hopefully Charlie would take her out in the yard to play.

"There's not much to tell. I applied to a handful of legal secretary jobs in Pittsburgh, a paralegal position in Atlanta, and an in-house corporate attorney in Denver."

"You don't sound excited about any of it."

"Law is not really my thing. It was my father's thing. And now, it's the only thing I feel qualified to do. I don't know." She shrugged. "Maybe family law would be nice. At least it's something remotely applicable to Charlotte. I mean, I'm a lot more interested in helping families than I am helping corporations these days."

"Atlanta is nice."

She'd never been.

"Will Charlotte split time between wherever you go and here?"

Morgan almost scoffed. Split time? She could barely get herself to leave her baby with Charlie for two hours. "No. Wherever I am, Charlotte will be, and I can't imagine Charlie protesting until she's much older. He's got the bistro to worry about."

"Still, I bet it will be hard for him when she leaves."

No doubt. It wouldn't be any easier on her and Charlotte.

There was something about Charlie that kept Morgan hanging on even when she was desperately telling herself to let go.

• • •

Charlie yelled when Charlotte bit down, trapping his finger between her teeth.

"Two-year-olds have teeth!"

"Of course they have teeth," Phyllis said. "How do you think she eats?"

His finger throbbed. Charlotte was like a freaking shark, but he managed to fish the rest of the play dough out of her mouth and deposit her on the kitchen floor while he cleaned up the mess. Even with Phyllis's help, his back ached and his breathing was hard. Had it really only been two hours since he'd gotten here?

Charlotte wailed.

Charlie lifted his brow in a pathetic beg as he turned to Phyllis. "What do I do?"

"She's just tired. I'll get her a sippy cup."

Charlotte pawed at his leg, and Charlie picked her up, but she reached for Phyllis instead.

"Uh-uh, little one. You can have your milk, but you stay with your daddy. I have a kitten to wrangle."

And then she was gone, out the back door, leaving Charlie with a sniveling, furiously sipping Charlotte. Now what?

He was screwed.

"Ssh, baby. Mommy will be home soon." He hoped. He didn't even know where Morgan was. That was probably a good thing. Otherwise, he and Charlotte may have crashed her party out of desperation.

As he walked to the living room, his little girl dropped her head to his chest. Her hand curled around his collar, and he melted.

Fortunately, the couch was nearby. He sat, and listened to her scattered breathing. The sippy cup dropped to the cushion beside him, but she never lost her grip on his shirt. He sighed, and rubbed his cheek against her fleshy knuckles. His nose ended up in her soft, strawberry-smelling hair.

There'd been an awful lot of turmoil in his life, but never—ever—peace like this.

His heartbeat slowed until his breaths matched hers, and he let his eyes close. On Phyllis Marion's ratty couch, with the biggest surprise of his life weighing on his chest, he felt like the luckiest man on earth.

The front door opened, and he startled to find Morgan staring at him.

Charlotte fidgeted, but as he smoothed a hand over her back, she settled again. Maybe he was dreaming.

"Hey," Morgan whispered. "You two look comfy. She ran you ragged, didn't she?"

Charlie lifted his chin above Charlotte's head. "It was fun."

"Good."

Her smile twinkled in her eyes. She was so damn pretty. And he was getting too damn comfortable in this fantasy world.

Morgan set her purse on the chair nearest the door.

"How was your … "

"Lunch? It was nice. I never really had a lot of time to get to know Mark before."

He tensed. She'd been with a guy, and not just any guy. "Mark Mitchell?" There went the fantasy.

"Yeah. He's helped me out a lot since I've been back. Apparently, he has a thing for the outcasts."

He hated the idea of Mark having any kind of thing for her.

She stepped closer, and after a pause, slipped her hands between them, separating their chests. "Here. Let me take her." She flipped Charlotte around and cradled her. "I'll be right back."

Why were the women in his life always tied up with Mitchells? First Morgan and Justin, then Alice and Justin, and now Morgan and Mark.

He pushed off the couch and headed home, thankful for the reality check. He wasn't going to be waiting on scraps from a Mitchell-Parrish relationship ever again.

Chapter Nine

Morgan had walked in on such a sweet moment yesterday—Charlotte cuddled against Charlie's chest and both of them asleep. She still didn't completely understand his abrupt departure afterward. Maybe it had something to do with her—or Mark.

That just complicated everything more than she needed, so even though she heard him banging around in the kitchen, preparing for the dinner crowd, she didn't stop to say hi or to tell him that Charlotte had been asking for him. This was not the time or place to work out the kinks in their twisted relationship.

She stuffed her purse in a locker and tied her apron around her waist. *Don't borrow trouble.* She had a roof over her head, an income, and cordial interactions with her child's father. That was enough.

But lately she was wishing for more. Just one touch, one taste, one night where she felt fully alive again.

She slammed the locker door.

"Hey now," Corbin said from behind her. "There's not a single person in that dining room, yet, so who caused your foul mood?"

His bowtie tilted, and Morgan reached out to give it a tweak. "I'm just mad at myself."

"For what?"

A pan clanged in the kitchen. "What do I need to do to get some help around here?" Charlie's voice ricocheted off the lockers.

Morgan hid a small sigh behind a smile. "Never mind. It's not a big deal. Go help Charlie before he blows a gasket."

After checking with Hannah about the evening's reservations and switching a few undesirable patrons to Corbin's side of the room, Morgan returned to the kitchen for her order tablet, which was updated with the new weekly menu.

"How's Charlotte?" Charlie asked. His back was to Morgan as he slid a tray of crostino into the holding rack.

A black T-shirt pulled across his shoulders, clinging to every undulation of his muscles. Air fluttered in her throat. "She's good. She was coloring when I left. Speaking of leaving … Why did you leave so fast, yesterday?"

Straightening, he glanced at her over his right shoulder. "I had someplace to be."

He disappeared into the pantry.

She growled. She couldn't figure him out. He was great with Charlotte, and he was good with her. But he could just as easily turn off the charm and walk away.

Ha! Well, she could do that, too.

With her order tablet in hand, Morgan left the kitchen. She was done trying to figure him out.

A few hours later, Mark walked into the restaurant. He'd been the one name on the reservation list that she was looking forward to.

"Good evening, Mrs. Mitchell." Morgan smiled. "Mark."

He pulled out his mother's chair.

When Margaret was seated, Morgan handed her the weekly menu. "Duck is back."

She wrinkled her nose. "I don't like slimy meat."

Laughter sputtered past Mark's lips.

His mother's shoulders shifted, and a thud sounded beneath the table.

His eyes went wide. "She kicked me."

Margaret stared at her menu as if she'd done nothing of the sort.

Morgan smirked. They were the oddest couple. "What can I get you to drink?"

When she had their drink order in hand, she headed for the beverage station, only to be summoned by table six.

"I asked for well done, not burned. I'd like another."

Ooh. That was not going to go over well with Charlie. "I'll see what I can do."

When Charlie saw the plate, he sneered. "The man asked for well-done; that's well done."

Morgan wrinkled her nose. It looked burnt. But questioning this cook could be like questioning a blood-thirsty king, and there were already enough headless bodies in this kitchen. Diplomacy. She used to be good at that when she'd wanted to be.

"Some people don't know anything about good cooking," she said.

"Damn straight." He threw another filet on the grill.

She was about to press her hands together in prayer formation when Corbin appeared and grabbed two plates off the serving counter.

"I served drinks to the Mitchells, and they're ready to order."

Charlie's posture stiffened. "Which Mitchells?"

Morgan clammed up.

"Mark and his mother are here," Corbin answered.

"Of course he is." Charlie glared at her. "Don't keep him waiting."

Morgan gaped at his back as he stalked into the pantry. He *was* jealous.

And whether she should be or not, she was smiling.

Once this restaurant was empty, they were going to have a little talk.

• • •

Charlie slammed a clean frying pan onto the overhead rack.

Fuck it. Whatever was going on between Morgan and Mark didn't matter. It certainly didn't matter enough to sabotage Mark's dish with an overdose of cayenne.

He pushed the pepper away. Morgan didn't belong to him now any more than she did back then. Charlotte, on the other hand, was his. He'd simply concentrate on that.

By the time service ended, Charlie had found his Zen again, scrubbing steel and glass until it shined.

"Good night," Corbin said, lifting a trash bag before he pushed through the alley door.

Charlie nodded. "See you tomorrow."

The door slammed shut, and Charlie stilled. Was Morgan here, or did she manage to sneak out with Hannah? She'd stayed away most of the evening, probably because he'd been grouchy. At least she didn't quit.

Morgan walked into the kitchen. "Did Corbin leave?"

Her hair was down, and she was missing the sweater she'd been wearing. Now, she was dressed in nothing but a tiny white T-shirt and black pants that fit her like a second skin.

Heat slithered around in his gut. "He's gone." Like she should be.

"Shoot. I wanted to split some tip money with him."

Charlie slid a carving knife into its case. "Keep it. You barely make anything in tips." The more tips she made, the faster she'd get out of town and out from under his skin.

"Well, I made plenty tonight. The Mitchells tipped me extra, and it's only fair Corbin gets half. He was at that table as much as I was."

Charlie stared at her for the longest time. *Don't go there.* It wasn't worth it. He had Charlotte, and she was way more than he ever expected.

"Why are you looking at me like that?"

"It's nothing."

"It's not nothing, Charlie. I know you well enough to know when you want to say something, but you won't let yourself."

"It's not worth saying."

"Say it anyway."

Why the hell not? He'd never held his tongue before. "Fine. I can't believe you're chasing after Mark Mitchell."

She had the nerve to grin. "I am not chasing after Mark."

He grunted. "Well then he's chasing after you. He's in this restaurant all the time, now. He's taking you to lunch on your day off. What would you call it?"

"Charlie, we're friends."

"That's what you said about Justin."

Her smile fell, and her face paled.

He felt like he'd flipped a switch, sending them back ten years, when suddenly her visits home from college, which he'd lived for, were complicated by her father's constant push for her to go somewhere and be someplace with Justin. Every time she'd cancelled on him for some swanky Parrish-Mitchell political affair, he'd handled the disappointment with a bottomless stiff drink.

"Charlie, listen to me." She stepped closer. "This is not the same thing. Mark is not a replacement for Justin. I'm not trying to replace Justin. I don't care about Justin. I never really did. I cared more about pleasing my father and the status that would come from being a politician's wife. That probably makes me the worst person in the world for agreeing to marry him in the first place. But it is what it is. I can't go back and change those things. All I can do is not make those same mistakes again."

Was he one of those mistakes? She'd tossed him aside like he was the trash everyone had said he was, the minute her daddy threatened to disown her. "What about me? Do you care about me? *Did* you care about me? Or was I just a thorn you liked to stab into your father's side?"

"No. You know that's not true. Before we broke up, I told you I loved you." Her voice rose sharply. "I can't believe you are questioning that!"

"Love? I don't think you had a fucking clue what the word meant. I sure as hell don't believe it applied to me. No, I was your entertainment. Sloppy drunk Charlie Cramer, always up for a good time when the pressures of being the Parrish princess weighed you down again." He shook his head. "I was such a sucker."

"No!"

"Then what was I to you?" he yelled. "And for once in your shitty life tell me the fucking truth."

"You were the only real thing in my life." Her finger jabbed at him through the air. "Everything else was so planned and calculated. Everything's worth was measured by how much money and power it made, or how good it looked. But you—you were—you—" She groaned, but when the sound faded, her eyes widened, as if she suddenly saw the truth. "You were the only thing I could *feel!*"

Silence fell over the kitchen. Nobody moved. He stared at her, so damn afraid to believe her words. Then he couldn't stand not touching her a minute more. He reached for her, running his hand up the warm, soft skin of her arm. When she closed her eyes, he reached for her other arm, sliding both hands upward until he cradled her neck.

His heart beat in his throat. "You have no idea what you do to me."

"You could show me." She slid her hands over his.

Charlie kissed her, fusing his lips to hers, holding her face at a slant, letting her exhalation warm his cheek. It was rough and hard and as distant as he could make it—just in case he got spooked and needed to walk away. He couldn't help but think one of them would. But then, he parted his lips just enough for his tongue to take the smallest taste. And that was it. Like the addict he was, he opened his mouth and swallowed her. Distance be damned.

Their mouths found a familiar rhythm slipping and sliding, opening and closing, probing and pulsing until he knew nobody was walking away without being well and truly fucked.

"Charlie," she whispered on her next breath. "I want you. I never stopped wanting you."

Somewhere in the back of his hazy head he knew what a person wanted wasn't always what he needed. But he didn't care. The desire ran too deep.

With his mouth covering hers and his arms holding on for dear life, he walked her backwards into his office.

She tugged at his pants. "Now, Charlie. I want you, now."

"Not now," he growled. "I'll tell you when." She'd been calling the shots in his life for way too long.

She hissed as he rolled the tip of his tongue over the curves of her ear to the base of her neck. Every muscle in his body swelled from the energy building inside of him.

He kept his mouth on her mouth and his hands on her body, ridding her of the T-shirt.

She stood before him with her hands clutching his waistband, dressed in a white lace bra that barely fit. So damn soft. He traced the mounding flesh. His pulse quickened, his groin tightened, and a spot beneath his ribs clenched.

Don't do it. She may want you now, but she'll leave in the end.

"Charlie," she whispered again. She pushed his T-shirt over his abs and lowered her lips to the skin above his navel. Her mouth doused his body in pricks of pleasure that made it mercifully hard to think. "I've missed you so much."

He closed his eyes and lifted his face to the ceiling while her breath tickled and her tongue teased. He smoothed his hands over her arms, her back, to the nape of her neck, where he threaded his fingers into her silky hair. Screw it. He'd take what he could take, because when it came to her he'd always been desperate.

It was then that he realized her mouth had stopped exploring, and her puffs of breath concentrated on one stretch of skin—the collection of numbers tattooed over his heart.

Dropping his chin to his chest, he looked at her looking up at him, a million questions in her eyes. *Don't answer her. Not if you want to survive this.*

He flipped her, bent her over his desk, and pulled her pants lower over the curves of her hips. He'd rather admire her ass than answer her questions. Answers were complicated. Sex was easy.

She wiggled against him, as brazen as she'd ever been, and he worked himself free. He wanted her—maybe even more than he'd ever wanted her before. So he was going to have her.

He'd never been any good at impulse control.

Gripping her hard around the soft waist, he slipped inside … and waited for his heart to start beating again.

• • •

Morgan braced herself against the desk and welcomed every blow. She wanted Charlie's thrusts to shake the sense right out of her. Because, otherwise, she might be absolutely, positively certain he still loved her. He had her birthdate tattooed on his chest. Over his heart. Right above Charlotte's birthdate.

Pleasure lifted a moan from her lips.

What if he did still love her? Would that change anything? Would that change this?

"Yes!" she screamed just to release some of the pressure.

He cupped her breasts, tightening her nipples until she yelled again.

It felt so good. Always had. When they'd been like this, they'd been perfect.

He reached between her legs and rubbed. She dropped her forehead to the desk and let the friction coax her orgasm. Time and place slipped away. There was just her … and him … like this.

When she shuddered, he groaned. And with one last thrust, he collapsed against her back, wrapping his arms around her waist and pulling her against him. The warm, luscious weight made her want to crumble to the floor and take him with her.

But then the haze cleared. The air chilled. And Charlie released her.

"I'm going to get cleaned up," he said.

She closed her eyes and swallowed the embarrassment-induced surge of acid. In the darkness behind her eyes, all she could see was the tattoo on his chest. He'd loved her right before she'd left town. Maybe he'd gotten the tattoo shortly after that.

It didn't mean he loved her now. Maybe he even regretted getting it.

And even if he did love her, it didn't magically fix anything. In their case, it always seemed to make things worse.

Chapter Ten

Charlie couldn't get the taste of Morgan out of his mouth or the feel of her off his skin. More than her birthdate was tattooed on his heart. Loving her was bound to kill him.

He glared at his reflection in the bathroom mirror. "Don't be so dramatic."

Just because he felt something, didn't mean he was going to die. He could handle this. Better than he'd handled everything else. Because this time, he wasn't going to drink over it.

And he wasn't going to be the one to walk away—even though he *was* the one hiding in the bathroom. *Pathetic.* He opened the door with a huff.

She stood at the end of the hall, wearing the shirt he'd removed, with a wide-eyed expression on her face.

Words stuck in his throat. Maybe he should've stayed in the bathroom a little longer. How was it possible to feel awkward around someone you knew well enough to have a child with?

"We kind of got carried away," she said.

He ran a hand over his head to the back of his neck. "We always do."

Her gaze wandered lower and seemed to linger on his chest. He wanted to scratch the hell out of the spot. If she asked about the tattoos, he could easily explain Charlotte's birthdate—he hadn't wanted to forget the child he was never supposed to meet. But Morgan's birthdate? He couldn't explain that without admitting he had always loved her, and he always would.

She lifted her purse onto her shoulder. "I don't want things to be weird between us."

"You mean weirder than they already were?"

"Exactly. So, I'm fine with pretending like whatever happened here didn't even happen."

He'd be good with that, too—if it were possible. "Okay."

She smiled. It wasn't the least bit flirty, but his engine revved. "Look at us being all mature."

Was that what you called it when you bent a woman over your desk and pounded into her like she was the last woman on earth? He swallowed his disgust. She'd always been better at pretending than he was.

He stretched his neck to either side. "You should probably get back to Charlotte." *Before I drag you into my office again.*

"Maybe you could come by the house to see her tomorrow?"

"Maybe." He shoved his hands into his jean pockets.

She was kidding herself if she thought they could pretend nothing happened.

"Okay." The alley door was behind her, and she stumbled as she walked backward. "I'll see you tomorrow."

Her voice quivered, and he grinned.

Even if he stayed away from Phyllis's house tomorrow, he'd still have to see Morgan again at work. She was everywhere. He had no doubt that was going to include tonight's dreams. He couldn't seem to get through an interaction with her unscathed.

At least he got out of this one without having to talk about the tattoos.

• • •

As Morgan drove out of town and up the windy road toward Aunt Phyllis's farmhouse, she couldn't suppress the tears. Through everything that had happened to her in the last three years, she'd rarely cried. Her parents' instruction in stoicism was too engrained. But tonight, she made up for it.

By the time she pulled into the dirt driveway, she wasn't even sure why she was crying. Was it because her father turned out to be a villain instead of the savior she'd been raised to believe he was? Was it because her mother, who was too cold and cowardly to care about her daughter, ran away, leaving Morgan to deal with the fallout from their transgressions? Was it because she was stuck here, where plenty of people enjoyed her misfortune? Or was it because of Charlie? Because she loved him, lost him, found him again—but it could never be the same?

The rush she used to feel from being with him against all odds and expectations wasn't there anymore. Now, she just felt raw ... and sad.

She stayed in the car long enough for the tears to dry, and then she walked with heavy steps across the porch and into the living room. Aunt Phyllis was sleeping in the recliner chair with her legs lifted and a kitten curled on her lap. This was what every second of every night had been like before Morgan and Charlotte roared into town. So lonely. What had chased Aunt Phyllis into this solitary life? Morgan didn't even know why her parents had been so adamant about staying away. Now, this woman they'd laughed at and ignored was all the family support Morgan had.

And Morgan loved her for it—more than she'd ever loved her parents.

"I'm home," she whispered. "Why don't you go up to bed?"

Aunt Phyllis's eyes fluttered open. "How was your night?"

"Exhausting." Physically and emotionally.

"Well, it's over now." She smiled. "Oh, before I forget. A man from Denver, Colorado called for you about a job. I wrote his number and his name beside the phone."

Snap. Just like that her exhaustion waned. "Seriously?"

Aunt Phyllis nodded and righted the chair, pushing the kitten from her lap. "And there's something else in the kitchen for you."

"What is it?" Morgan raised a brow.

"Go see."

It really didn't matter what it was, a job possibility was all Morgan needed to feel hopeful again. With any luck, she could get out of here and get on with her plan to build a life Charlotte could be proud of.

On her way to the kitchen, she stopped at the phone and peered at the notepad. Johnson Berger. She didn't recognize the name. She would have to go through her records of the jobs she'd applied to.

"Did you see it?" Aunt Phyllis asked.

"Yeah, but I'm not sure which job this is."

"I wasn't talking about that." She pointed across the room. "I was talking about *that*."

In the dim light from above the stove, she saw a plate piled high with heart-shaped sugar cookies. The tops of the pink-iced cookies distorted against the plastic wrap, but still she could see the letters "P," "M," "C," and "D".

"We decorated one for me, one for you, one for Charlotte, and one for Charlie," Aunt Phyllis said. "But baby girl refused to make a 'C' for Charlie, because, 'He Daddy.' How 'bout that?"

Morgan raised fingers to her lips and sighed. "How sweet." That was going to make Charlie's day.

"Definitely sweet, but messy, too. *Woo wee!* That child is like a tornado." Aunt Phyllis chuckled. "But I love her, like I love you." She wrapped an arm around Morgan's shoulders and pulled her into a hug.

God, it felt good to hear those words and to have someone to come home to at the end of a long night. The tears tingled in her eyes again.

"We're blessed," Aunt Phyllis said. "Very blessed."

Those words played in Morgan's head as she readied for bed, watching her baby girl sleeping in the double bed Aunt Phyllis had pushed against the wall the day they'd arrived. That day,

Morgan hadn't *felt* blessed, and she hadn't thought Aunt Phyllis *looked* blessed living a life like this.

"But how could I not be blessed, when I have you?" Morgan snuggled up against Charlotte.

To think she ever thought adoption was the only answer. How cold and empty would life be without her baby girl?

She'd be like Aunt Phyllis—before they'd come to town.

The sadness returned. Whoever Johnson Berger was, he had a potential job for her. In Denver. She didn't know anyone in Denver, and Colorado was a long way from Pennsylvania. Wasn't that what she wanted?

She didn't know anymore.

Morgan reached out to stroke her daughter's hair. "As long as I have you, I'll be fine." But she wondered if Aunt Phyllis and Charlie thought the same thing when they looked at Charlotte.

The next day, Morgan and Charlotte enjoyed a couple plain sugar cookies while they sat on the front porch glider. The special, frosted ones were waiting to be eaten if and when Charlie showed up.

Morgan glanced at her watch. With the time difference, it was still too early to call Denver, but it was almost time to feed the chickens that were gathering at Charlotte's feet in search of crumbs.

The chickens scattered when a shiny car rustled the gravel drive. *Mark.* She frowned, but covered it with another bite. She would rather see Charlie.

"Hey," she said as he emerged from the car.

"Hey." He smiled brightly at Charlotte. "Hey, kiddo."

Charlotte tried to stand, and the glider shuddered. Morgan reached behind her and swung the little one up on her hip before she took a tumble. "This is a surprise."

"Ladies' bible study. Once again, I have a couple hours to kill."

With me. Which seemed more and more curious after Charlie pointed it out. How did Mark kill time before she'd come to town?

"We were about to officially feed the chickens." Morgan brushed cookie crumbs off Charlotte's shirt. "You're welcome to join us."

Mark agreed, but he looked like he might be having second thoughts as he picked a careful path through the high grass in the backyard. "You had a dramatic evening last night."

She hid a shocked expression behind Charlotte's head. He had no idea how dramatic. Her face heated on thoughts of Charlie. "You think? I thought it was pretty routine."

"Well, somebody or something was always pulling you away from our table and leaving us with Corbin. Not that I minded."

Was he being possessive? She hoped not. She needed a friend more than she needed an admirer.

After slipping into the shed and grabbing a bucket of feed, she settled Charlotte onto the rusted tractor. "We're friends, right?"

He nodded as he leaned against a rickety wood fence, but the minute a chicken skirted his feet, he straightened. "Of course we are."

"Nothing more, right?"

He laughed, but the laugh caught in his throat as he sidestepped more chickens. "Why do you ask?"

"Well, because Charlie thought I was after you or you were after me. I'm just making sure neither one of us was or is after the other."

Mark looked at Charlotte, who was cackling as she made it rain chicken feed. "No offense, but you're not my type."

"Twenty-five pounds, a good haircut, and a Chanel suit ago I was everyone's type." She redirected Charlotte's hand to keep the feed away from Mark.

"I think you look great. I just think guys look better."

Her brows lifted. Mark was gay? She'd been minutes away from marrying into the Mitchell family, and she'd never had a clue. She wondered if any of them had. "Seriously?"

He nodded. "You know, maybe I should wait on the porch?" He backed away from the tractor, lifting and shaking his feet to scare chickens as he went.

Typical Mitchell. She laughed.

Once the chickens were fed and Charlotte was cleaned and busy with Aunt Phyllis inside, Morgan walked Mark to his car.

"So, you're gay," she said. "Is this common knowledge, and I'm just slow, or is it a secret?"

"I wouldn't say it's common knowledge, but it's not exactly a secret either. My mother knows. A few years after high school, I said, 'I'm gay.' And she said, 'I know.'" He laughed. "But we never really talked about it again."

Huh. Morgan didn't know what to think about Margaret's reaction. "Does she accept and support you?"

He shrugged. "In her own way, yes. Honestly, I think she's just happy I won't be dragged away from her by some woman like Justin and Will have been. She's got this thing about being alone."

"What happens when you find someone?"

"I don't know. In an ideal world, he'd like being around her as much as I do. That's probably a tall order. I guess I'm going to find out soon. Corbin and I are going to the movies and dinner in Rileyville on Sunday."

Morgan's jaw dropped. Corbin was gay, too? Quirky, yes, but gay? "So that's who's bringing you into the bistro."

"Guilty. It's not easy for a semi-closeted gay man to find someone in a small town. And when he does, he doesn't want to lose him."

She grinned. "And *that's* why you're so concerned about the possibility of the bistro closing." He nodded, and she laughed. "Well, I think you two will make a great couple. Honest to God,

I can't think of two guys I like more." Not including Charlie of course.

He grabbed her hand and squeezed. "Thank you."

Later, as she watched him drive away, satisfaction bubbled in her chest. He wasn't after her. Her laughter carried on the breeze. Better yet, she had a friend, a good friend, who trusted her with something pretty big.

It'd been a long time since anyone trusted her like that.

"Morgan, Mr. Berger is on the phone for you."

She shot a puzzled look at Aunt Phyllis. Why was he calling again so soon? She hadn't even had a chance to return his last call.

With a smile on her face, she headed toward the house. Who knew? By the end of the day she could have a good friend *and* a new job.

Her smile faded. Too bad she'd have to lose one to claim the other.

• • •

Charlie stood inside Alice's old bedroom, surveying the gritty subfloor. Ripping out that matted shag carpet had been a ball-busting feat, but now he could picture something else in here: a bedroom for Charlotte.

He imagined pale yellow walls and a soft blue ceiling. With clouds. He'd buy a crib. Did she still sleep in a crib? He roughed a palm over his mouth. He'd buy new bedding for Alice's old twin bed, too. That way Charlotte could grow into the space.

Maybe he'd even sleep in here once or twice—just to hear her breathing.

Idiot. She doesn't live with you. He shook his head. Maybe not, but he was going to make a place in his life for her just the same. He'd never felt like his father wanted him. He was going to make damn sure Charlotte never doubted how much he loved her.

"My goodness! It sure is easy to erase someone's memory."

Alice. She was always so melodramatic. "I couldn't erase you if I tried … and I've tried."

She stood in the doorway with her hands braced on the jamb. Gaudy bracelets dangled from both wrists. "Ha! Well, I should get veto power over whatever you have planned for my new room. A man cave with a big screen and a recliner chair is not a reasonable way to pay me homage."

Charlie's gut jumped. Alice would like anything that had to do with Morgan even less. "It's not your house anymore, remember?" He pushed by her and headed down the hall toward the living room.

"Ohhhkaaaay. What did I say wrong? You're kind of pissy."

She'd be pissy too if she were trying to convince herself something major that happened last night didn't happen. "I'm not pissy. I'm just busy. I need to finish this renovation so I can stop choking on sawdust."

"Charlie, look at me." Alice grabbed onto his wrist and tugged.

When he turned, she stared at him with the same worried eyes she'd leveled on him when he'd been drinking. *Damn it!* He couldn't be spared the speculation even when he was painfully sober.

"I'm fine, Alice."

"Is this about Morgan?"

His hand fisted as he broke from her grip. "No, this is about Charlotte." Regret set in the minute he closed his mouth.

"What about Charlotte? Is she okay?"

"She's fine. Everything is fine. I'm just … I want to turn your old room into a nursery."

Alice's eyes bulged. "Why? She doesn't live with you. She's not going to live with you." She shook her head until her crazy curls scattered. "Do not tell me you're moving them in here."

God, he wished. He could see Morgan holding a sleeping Charlotte in the living room. He could even see her making macaroni and cheese on his three-thousand-dollar range. His pulse hammered. "You need to calm the hell down." He walked into the kitchen and yanked a bottle of soda from the fridge.

"Gladly, just tell me they aren't going to live here, and nothing is going on with you and Morgan."

He wrenched the cap free, and let the soda barrel down his throat until it landed hard in the pit of his stomach. He didn't have to tell Alice anything.

Closing the fridge, he walked away from her again. "I have work to do. You can leave unless you plan on picking up a hammer."

"Oh my God!" She raced past him, blocking the entrance to the hallway. "They're moving in here. You're falling for her again."

He spun on her. "They are *not* moving in here. I just want my daughter to have a place to stay if she needs it. I want her to feel wanted." He growled. "I'm trying to be a good dad—something we never had. You of all people should be happy about it."

Her shoulders sagged. "You're right. I want you to be a good dad. I just don't want you to get hurt again." She patted his chest. "Love your little girl, but protect your heart, Charlie. No matter what. Morgan is a runner. She's not going to stay in Harmony Falls, and who can blame her, right? Not us. We know how hard it is to be the outcast."

Hell, he was still trying to overcome that. "I get it, Alice. Now, will you please move?"

She stepped aside, and he walked down the hall only to stop when she called out to him.

Just once he'd like to have the last word. "What?"

"She's a Parrish, too, remember. She might be down and out now, but she won't always be. And even if she could get past all the gossip around here, I can't imagine her ever being happy living a simple life like this."

His jaw clenched. "With a simple man, like me."

"Charlie, that's not what … "

"That's exactly what you meant." He shook his head and rolled his eyes. "You say you want me sober, but you sure as hell are aggravating me enough to make me want a drink."

"Don't say that."

"Why not? It's true. And you know what else is? You haven't asked to see your niece once since she's been here. I think that sucks. You of all people would get a kick out of seeing her. She looks like you."

Alice smirked. "Really?"

He nodded. "Really."

"It's not that I don't want to see her."

"You just don't want to see Morgan."

"That makes me sound terrible." She sighed.

"So don't be terrible. Go see your niece, and cut her mother some slack."

Charlie wasn't holding his breath. It would take an act of God to get those two in the same room together again.

Chapter Eleven

Morgan awoke to the sound of someone getting sick in the bathroom down the hall. Charlotte was sleeping soundly beside her. For a change, it wasn't her with the virus.

Bonus. Except, Morgan had to work tonight. A sick Aunt Phyllis couldn't take care of a little girl.

Pushing the covers away and tip-toeing from the bedroom, Morgan checked on Aunt Phyllis and then helped her back to bed.

"Don't bother with me." The clearly miserable woman tried to shoo her away. "I've been taking care of myself for fifty years."

Morgan wrinkled her face. That sounded like such a horrible way to live. "Well, then, you're long overdue for a break." She pulled the covers to Aunt Phyllis's chin. "I'll check on you in a little bit."

A few hours later, Charlotte was up, fed, and bathed, and Morgan needed to call Charlie. Her heart jumped at the thought of asking for the night off from work. Probably a residual reflex from all the times she'd called off in Connecticut. Whatever it was, she was going to have to get past it. This was only a trial run, anyway.

She was going to need a lot more than one night off if the phone interview she'd agreed to after talking with Mr. Berger resulted in a trip to Denver.

"Hello." Charlie's gravelly voice hinted at sleep.

"Did I wake you?"

"It's no big deal. I was up late working on the house."

Maybe that's why he'd never shown up or called yesterday. She hoped. Because the longer she went without seeing him, the harder it was to convince herself they could act like nothing had happened between them in his office.

"What's up?" he asked.

"Aunt Phyllis is sick. She can't watch Charlotte, so I have to call off." Her stomach tossed like she was in Connecticut all over again.

He sighed. "You know, Hannah's going to quit again if I try to put her on the tables, and Corbin can't serve everyone. Maybe Alice could watch Charlotte."

"Nope." *Alice Cramer Mitchell is not getting six unsupervised hours to poison my daughter against me.*

"You and my sister need to get over your issues, so my daughter can get to know all of her family."

Morgan could do without Charlotte knowing that part. "Does Alice even know how to take care of a toddler?"

"Did Aunt Phyllis before you showed up?"

A low growl gurgled in her throat. He had a point. "I don't know, Charlie."

"I need you at the restaurant. If Charlotte were sick, it would be a different story. But she's not, and Alice is not a mass murderer. She's perfectly capable of taking care of a child."

Morgan didn't know how to argue that. Charlotte wasn't sick. Alice wasn't a murderer. And Charlie *needed* her. Her neck warmed. That sounded so good. It probably shouldn't *feel* this good, though. Not if they were supposed to be pretending like nothing ever happened. "You don't even know if Alice is available tonight."

"I'll call her."

"Fine."

With any luck, Alice would be busy.

Five hours later, Morgan pulled into the last place on earth she ever thought she'd be: her ex-fiancé's driveway. *At least Justin was still at work,* she told herself as she glanced in the rearview mirror at a sleeping Charlotte. She didn't want to face him again after he'd turned down her request for a job and she'd been the reason he was kicked out of the bistro.

Seeing Alice after all that was bad enough.

Speaking of the devil ... the front door opened, and Alice stepped onto the porch.

Morgan took a deep breath. She could do this. Charlie needed her at the restaurant, and Charlotte needed to spend time with her aunt. *Don't be selfish.* "Time to wake up, sweetie."

Pushing out of the car, Morgan nodded at Alice, but a smile wouldn't form. "Thank you for agreeing to this."

"I'm here when Charlie needs me."

Hmm. How was she supposed to take that comment? Was it a dig at Morgan for leaving town and refusing to see Charlie when he followed? Was it a reminder that Alice was doing this for him and not Morgan? She opened her mouth to challenge Alice, but snapped it shut instead.

Quit looking for something to fight about. She hoisted a sleepy Charlotte onto her shoulder, and started the painful march toward Justin and Alice's front porch.

"You can lay her on the guest bed if you think she'll stay sleeping for a bit." Alice held the screen door open.

Charlotte's head popped up.

"Hey, angel," Alice cooed. "Oh my God, aren't you sweet! She does look like me."

Morgan bit her tongue—for Charlotte's sake ... for Charlie's sake, too.

This being unselfish thing wasn't easy.

"We're going to have so much fun." Alice clapped. "We're going to sing and dance and play dress ups. She's too young for makeup, right?"

"Way too young."

"Gog," Charlotte yelled as she opened and closed her hand toward the screen door, where Alice's dog, Mouse, stood. "Me see gog."

Forget the makeup. Charlotte wouldn't need anything but Mouse to have a good time. "She's very fond of animals."

Alice kept her overly enthusiastic face trained on Charlotte. "Mouse is the best doggy ever. Come to Auntie Alice and we'll go say hi."

"Me see gog," Charlotte said again, practically jumping from Morgan's arms to Alice's.

Ugh. That hurt, even though the show of enthusiasm was more for the dog than for Alice. She followed Alice up the steps and set the diaper bag in the foyer, uncomfortable in her surroundings.

Charlotte and Mouse got acquainted in the spotless, impeccably decorated living room. This place was going to be a mess by the time Charlotte was through. Morgan smiled.

"I'll be back for her around ten, maybe earlier." The dog was only going to keep Charlotte distracted for so long. Eventually she was going to realize she was in a strange place with a strange lady, and mama was nowhere around. "Charlie said we'll see how it goes, and I might be able to shorten my shift. Of course, if you need me before then, just call."

"She'll be fine." Alice stared at Morgan, and for a second it seemed like she had something more to say, but then she nodded and squatted beside Charlotte and Mouse. "Tell Mama 'See ya later.'"

After a few tears, Morgan slipped out of the house, leaving her daughter behind. She hoped she wouldn't regret this.

• • •

Charlie looked up from the paper products order form when he heard the alley door open and close. *Morgan.* Corbin and Hannah were already in the dining room, setting up for service, so who else would it be?

His pulse kicked up. *Ask about Charlotte—nothing more.* Because nothing more was supposed to have happened.

It took longer than he expected for her shadow to darken the hallway, and when she walked by, it was practically a sprint.

"Hey." He stood.

"Yeah?" She stayed somewhere down the hall.

"Can you come in here?"

Silence.

Maybe he should've gone out there to make it "less weird." Charlie shook his head and stepped toward the door. He'd never been any good at playing games like this.

She appeared. "What's up?"

"How'd it go with Charlotte and Alice?"

"Good." Her pretty face reddened as she looked around the room behind him. "I'm actually surprised it went so well." Her gaze settled on him. "Either Alice and I have matured *a lot*, or you threatened to burn down her theater."

He chuckled. "I didn't threaten her. I asked nicely."

"Ooh! Now look who's maturing." She grinned. "I always knew you had it in you, Charlie Cramer."

He flashed a not-so-innocent smile, and—*zap!*—something hot and strong laced the air between them.

She must've felt it, too, because she stepped back. "I should go. Help Corbin and Hannah."

She was going to pretend like nothing happened there, too.

"Hold on." He grabbed her wrist, and she froze. "This is not working for me."

"What isn't?" she whispered.

He let her go and stepped back into his office, crooking his finger. "Come in here and close the door."

Her eyes rounded, but then her lips twitched. "Ask me nicely."

"Please."

Morgan followed him into the office, but she kept her back glued to the closed door. "Charlie, I want you … "

He raised a hand to cut her off. "I like that sentence."

She gave him a cocky look. "There was more to that sentence."

"There doesn't need to be." He stepped forward, touching the tips of his boots to the tips of her shiny black shoes, and then he leaned in until their bodies brushed. "I can't pretend like nothing is happening."

"Me neither." She wrapped her arms around him and covered his mouth with hers.

Immediately, the door shook on a knock, and they broke apart. "Chef, the produce delivery guy is here."

"I'll be right there," Charlie called.

"Okay. Should I call Morgan? She's late."

Morgan covered her mouth as Charlie smirked and tucked a hand between her legs, slowly drawing his thumb over her core with firm pressure.

He barely held in a chuckle. "Nope. I'm sure she's coming."

"You are so bad," she whispered.

He bobbed his eyebrows and kissed her again.

Fifteen minutes later and behind on dinner prep, Charlie realized his escarole order was filled with kale instead.

Are you kidding me? He stabbed a knife into a cutting block just as Hannah walked into the kitchen. "Get me Furhman's Farm and Market on the fucking phone right now."

The teen looked scared to death.

"I'll do it." Morgan appeared behind Hannah and patted her on the back. She tossed a raised-brow look at Charlie after Hannah walked away. "That poor girl just wanted to use the bathroom."

"Well, I just wanted escarole." He shook a bunch of kale. "You tell him I never agreed to substitutions."

She rolled her eyes. "Where's the phone number?"

"On the order form on my desk."

"I'll take care of it."

And she did.

Twenty minutes later a hulking blonde kid dropped off escarole.

"He said his dad said you can keep the kale," Morgan said. "Oh, and your next order is half off."

Charlie checked to make sure it was escarole, first, and then he smiled at her. "Thanks. Moe would've told me to go to hell."

She smiled back. "That's because you would've called him a bastard."

"Probably. I don't know want happens to me, but when something goes wrong around here, I freak. I hate dealing with the business crap. I just want to cook."

"Well, I like it. Spreadsheets and conversation sort of turn me on." She winked.

Hot damn! "I got a shitload of spreadsheets in my office. Have at 'em."

"Maybe I will. Maybe I'll start coming in early."

She left him with the biggest smile on his face.

Three hours later, with things finally back on track, she walked into the kitchen, opened the refrigerator, and bent over to reach the bottom shelf. That ass. It was going to get him into trouble again.

She caught him staring as she straightened. "What are you looking at, Chef?"

"Some mighty fine rump roast."

"*That* was cheesy."

He couldn't stop laughing.

When he finally turned his attention back to the salmon he'd been searing, it was black. *Shit.* Charlie threw the pan, complete with ruined fish, into the sink, making a horrible racket.

"Whoa. Is everything okay?" Corbin grabbed two plates from the warming rack.

"It's fine. She just needs to stay the hell out of the kitchen." But he didn't mean it. "I'm easily distractible when she's around. I need to work on that." He grinned.

Corbin's jaw dropped.

"What?"

"You're smiling … in the kitchen." He glanced at the roof. "Is the sky falling?"

"Out, smart ass."

By nine o'clock, things had slowed down. One more table to serve, and it wasn't Morgan's.

Standing at the stove, Charlie couldn't see her, but he could hear the clanging of dirty dishes as she placed them in the holding sink. As much as he wanted her here after closing, her mind was elsewhere. "You should go. I know you're worried about Charlotte."

"I'm not worried. I'm … Okay, I'm a little worried."

He glanced over his shoulder and saw she'd moved closer to him. "Go. Corbin, Hannah, and I can handle things from here."

"Thank you." A rush of warm air hit his back before he felt her body brush against his. Her lips landed just below his ear. "Good night."

He needed a cold shower—and maybe one of those dorky aprons that read "Kiss the Cook." Because he sure as hell could get used to "thank yous" and "good nights" like that.

• • •

Pulling into Alice and Justin's driveway should've been easier the second time around. But the luxury car parked on the far side of the pavement had her throat closing. Justin was here.

But Charlotte was here, too. *That* was what mattered.

Tonight had been her best night at the bistro, and she wasn't going to squander her good mood because she was too afraid to face her past. *Be brave.*

Justin met her at the door, pushing open the screen. "Everywhere I go, there you are." He didn't look happy about it, but still he stepped aside and waved her in.

"I'm sorry about that." She was starting to feel like a broken record. "My aunt is sick, and I didn't have anywhere else to turn."

He shook his head. "Question: had I gone through with the wedding were you going to pass her off as mine?"

She flinched. She'd asked herself that question a million times. "I don't know what I would've done. Thank God it didn't come to that."

Justin had never been the kind of guy who lost his cool, and despite her answer that didn't happen now. He just sort of stood there glaring at her, but whatever he was thinking stayed locked inside. "She's sleeping in the family room on the couch." He turned and walked away.

Was she supposed to follow? She waited a few beats before she headed off in the same direction.

"We put cushions on the floor in case she rolled. Plus, I've been sitting on the floor in front of her watching the ball game for the last hour."

Her heart pinched. He wasn't at all comfortable with this situation, but he was trying. "Thank you," she said.

He shrugged. "She's an easy kid."

"She is, but, I know it can't be easy to have her here—or me for that matter."

He shoved his hands into his pockets. "I might not trust you or like what you did, but it doesn't make sense to punish a child." He pointed to the couch. "She's my niece. And her father is my friend."

Charlotte's chubby cheek squished against a flannel sheet someone had laid beneath her.

Morgan blinked back tears. He was right. Charlotte didn't deserve to be punished for any of this. She deserved the best life Morgan could give. "She's out cold."

"And I'm about to follow." Alice appeared at the mouth of the hallway, wearing pink, men's style pajamas. "We played like crazy. Danced like maniacs." Sans the usual layers of makeup and with a headband pulling her curls away from her face, she looked sweet. Certainly less bitchy than she'd always been toward Morgan.

"Babe." Justin sidled up beside his wife. "I have to call Will." He planted a kiss on Alice's temple. "Goodnight, Morgan." And then he disappeared down the hall.

Uncle Justin. That was so much easier to swallow than *husband* would've been.

Morgan glanced at Charlotte and smiled. Her baby's extended family was fraught with drama, but at least this side hadn't ended up in jail.

"She was really good—ate all her dinner." Alice said. "Well, she ate what she didn't feed to Mouse. But trust me, he wasn't complaining."

"Thank you."

"I did it for Charlie."

A chill picked at Morgan's skin. There it was again—that response that had Morgan looking for the double meaning. "Alice, you are Charlotte's aunt, and I don't want bad blood between us. I'm happy you got to spend time with her tonight. And, I'm happy for you and Justin. I really am."

"You think my concerns are about your connection to Justin?" She shook her head. "No. That's ancient history. My concerns are about your connection to Charlie. That's his past, present, and future now that you have a daughter together. You've always wreaked havoc on his life."

Morgan tensed. Charlie was a grown man. He didn't need his baby sister protecting him. "All I want is for Charlotte to know and love her daddy. And really, how that happens is none of your concern. Charlie and I can manage the details of raising our daughter." She bent to pick up her little girl.

"I'm worried he's drinking again."

He couldn't be. Sure, she'd had similar thoughts once or twice since she'd been back, but she'd been spending at least six hours a day, five days a week with him, and she hadn't so much as caught a whiff of liquor or heard the slightest slur. "Why would you say that?" She straightened and glared at Alice.

"He's under a lot of stress between the bistro ... and you. I caught him at the house holding a shot of whiskey."

Morgan gasped. *No!* The last thing she ever wanted to do was push Charlie to drink again. "When?"

"Right after you showed up. He said he wasn't going to drink it, but still ... "

"He came close." Her stomach pushed into her throat. How many times had he come close again since she'd been here?

"I have no idea what's happening when I'm not there. So, you see? Your history with my husband is the least of my worries. I love my niece, but she's a package deal with you. And as long as you're around, my brother is at risk."

Damn it. She didn't want to believe that was true. But wasn't that exactly why she hadn't contacted him when she'd decided to keep the baby? She'd refused to be the reason he started drinking again.

"Mama?" A bleary-eyed Charlotte stirred and sat up. Turning away from Alice, Morgan scooped Charlotte into her arms. "Mommy's here, baby girl." Her voice was shaking. "Thank you for watching her."

It wouldn't happen again. Morgan was getting out of Harmony Falls, before she destroyed Charlie for good.

Chapter Twelve

Charlie snapped the cover on the bowl of lentil tabouli and set it aside. He glanced at the clock. Tonight, Morgan was truly late for work—and unfortunately not because she was pressed against his office door.

Service started in a half hour.

"Hey, Corbin, can you try calling Phyllis's house again?"

Charlie needed to keep his mind on the food. He had his first fully booked service since the bistro opened, and a waiter-in-training to boot. He'd be damn ecstatic if he had a hostess and three wait staff, covering a full house.

"Still no answer," Corbin said as he hung up the phone and wrapped an apron around his waist. "I'll try her again after I set up the water glasses."

An image of Alice popped into Charlie's head, bearing a grin and a message: *She's a runner.*

"Shut up." He unleashed his frustration with a mallet on some duck breast.

Morgan's appearance a few minutes later startled him. She blew into the kitchen and reached for her apron.

"I'm sorry I'm late. I … wanted to make sure dinner was cooked and everything was settled before I left. Aunt Phyllis still isn't feeling one-hundred percent, and Charlotte was a bit cranky." She didn't look at him.

"Alice could've watched her again."

Morgan's entire body jerked as she yanked the strings of the apron around her waist. "No need."

She damn near sprinted into the dining room.

Huh. Charlie stared at the empty space where Morgan had been standing. What the hell was that? *That* was completely opposite from the way last night had started.

He wielded the mallet with such enthusiasm the metal prep space shook.

Alice had sworn to him everything went well between them, but something wasn't right with Morgan. He'd have to pull it out of her later on, when the evening calmed down.

Unfortunately, that didn't look like it was going to happen until after closing.

Charlie's first clue that trouble was brewing in the dining room came from Corbin. "Your presence is requested at table three." He huffed. "The new kid told a lady that he'd check with you about vegan options. I told him—and then I told her—there were no vegan options or substitutions. She claims that policy discriminates against her spiritual beliefs. She'd like to talk to you."

"Are you fucking kidding me?"

"Afraid not. Table three."

The new kid better be able to tolerate yelling.

Fortunately, by the time Charlie made it out to the dining room, the herbivore had hightailed it outta there. He wasn't complaining. He'd rather lose a table that didn't understand his food than compromise a dish so someone would stay.

But before he could settle into a rhythm again, Corbin had returned. "Is there a full moon, Chef?"

Charlie laughed, but he didn't feel happy. "I have no idea. Why?"

"Now, there's some old bat giving Morgan a hard time at table eight. I offered to switch tables with her, but she said not to make it a big deal."

Charlie closed his eyes, but quickly refocused on the plate he'd been garnishing. "Then don't make it a big deal." *And I won't either.*

A few minutes later, Morgan stepped into the kitchen to fill her tray.

"Is everything okay?" he asked.

"Fine."

How did she get the word past those clenched teeth?

A groan rumbled in his chest. *Don't do it. Do not follow her into that dining room.* He finally had a full house and a damn-near full wait staff.

But when he heard the sound of breaking glass, he had no choice.

"You are a clumsy fool." The shrill female voice made him wince.

Morgan dropped to the floor amid pieces of broken plates, and that gave Charlie a chance to see who'd made the insult: Pamela Boardman, Margaret's good friend.

Shit. Everyone was gawking and pointing at the scene of the crime. Charlie walked across the dining room to squat beside Morgan and pick up shards of porcelain. "Accidents happen."

"Go," she whispered. He would've missed her plea had he so much as exhaled.

Pamela stomped her feet inches from Charlie's hand. "All you have to say for your establishment and its wait staff is 'accidents happen'? Your judgment is no better sober."

Charlie pinched a piece of glass hard enough to draw blood. What a bitch. He glared at the prune-faced woman.

But she didn't back down. "Why is a Parrish even working here? A month ago, her father was arrested, and just today they doubled the charges against him, arrested her uncle, and launched an investigation against her mother. It's incredulous that you're still letting her work here. She's as corrupt as the rest of them. You mark my word. They'll arrest her next."

Morgan dropped the plate she'd been holding and scrambled off to the kitchen.

Pamela looked down her nose at Charlie. "That woman should be fired and forced to pay for my food, and Margaret should shut you down."

He fisted his hands. After this, Margaret probably would shut him down. Might as well go out with a bang. "Mrs. Boardman … " he stood, "Morgan doesn't need to pay for your food, because you're not getting any. If you were the last hungry mouth on earth, I'd let you starve."

Gasps sounded around him. He was surprised he could hear them over his raging heartbeat. "New Kid … " he snapped his fingers, "grab a broom and clean up that mess. Corbin, show these people out. We're closed. They can try the Main Street Diner."

He sure as hell didn't feel like cooking. And that was a first.

Storming into the kitchen, he looked for Morgan, but she was gone.

Blood throbbed in his neck veins, and his vision blurred. She probably went home. He wished she hadn't left before he could calm her down.

He grabbed his keys off the hook inside his office door.

"Charlie, maybe I could cook for everyone?" Corbin stood in the hallway. "The new kid can wait tables, and Hannah can keep hostessing."

"I don't care what you do."

Right now, the only thing Charlie cared about was finding Morgan.

· · ·

Morgan stared in horror at the newspaper she had spread out over the steering wheel. Everything that awful woman said was true. There were new charges against her father. They'd finally found Uncle Harold. But not her mother. As a result, a warrant had been issued for her arrest.

Her entire family was going to be in jail before this investigation was through. Morgan would have to spend God only knew how many years explaining to Charlotte why grandma and grandpa's Christmas cards came postmarked from a federal prison.

She smashed up the newspaper and tossed it into the backseat.

What was Johnson Berger going to think of this? The interview with him and his human resources manager had gone so well this afternoon that it ran an hour over and made her late for work. She was sure she'd get the job. *Well forget that.* They were probably watching the evening news right now, making the connection between the felonious Parrishes and their top candidate's last name.

On a squeal of tires, she left the gas station parking lot. Barreling up Main Street, she passed her old house. It looked so damned perfect on the outside—just like her family had looked. Too bad nobody knew the truth about what had been happening behind closed doors until it was too late.

Pamela's words resounded. *You mark my words. They'll arrest her next.*

Morgan choked on the saliva pooling in her mouth. She couldn't be arrested for something she didn't do, could she? She'd already talked to the authorities when her father was first arrested. They'd never pursued her again.

But what if they did? The prison system was filled with innocent people. *Oh, God.* What would happen to Charlotte? At least she'd have Charlie. And Aunt Phyllis, too. Suddenly, coming back to Harmony Falls didn't seem so bad.

Morgan swiped the back of her hand across her dripping nose and floored the gas pedal, heading up the hill and out of town toward Aunt Phyllis's house. The daytime running lights glistened on the wet street. She needed to get to Charlotte.

As long as she had her baby girl, everything would be fine.

The road straightened out, but she didn't reduce her speed. When she glanced at the speedometer, it registered seventy-five. In a thirty-five-mile-per-hour zone. *Don't be stupid.*

She eased up on the gas pedal and refocused on the road just in time for a deer to dart into her path.

"Shit!" Squeezing the steering wheel, she yanked it hard to the left. Thank God, she missed it.

But there was nothing she could do about the tree.

• • •

About a mile outside of town, Charlie came upon Morgan's mangled car. The passenger side door was crushed against a tree trunk.

His heart rate exploded in an uneven beat. *Holy shit!* Was she hurt?

"Morgan!" He yelled before he was even out of the car.

In a dead sprint, he reached the driver's side. The air bags had deployed, and the passenger window glass scattered over the seats, but Morgan wasn't there.

He took a moment to let that sink in. She'd walked away. That was good.

The longer he sat with that, the more his breathing evened. And when he finally looked up over the roof of the car, she was coming toward him.

"Jesus! Are you okay?" He ran to her.

"I swerved to miss a deer." Her upper lip was fat and bleeding, and a bright red split slashed across her cheek. "I hit the tree instead. I probably would've been better off hitting the deer." She wiped at a tear and winced.

Relief yanked a laugh from his chest. "Don't touch your face." He grabbed her hands and inspected them for damage. "You could have slivers of glass anywhere."

Her shoulders sagged, and the tears poured. "My car is totaled."

"Better the car than you." He pulled her gently against him.

Her fingers dug into his biceps. "I was just so upset. She said … I thought … I didn't know what to do. So I ran."

He smoothed her hair. "Yeah, you're good at that." Normally, that would've pissed the hell out of him. Right now, he just wanted to hold her.

"I need to see Charlotte. I don't want to lose her."

"You're not going to lose her. Everything's going to be fine. I'll take you to her, but first we need to get you checked out and this mess cleaned up."

While Morgan used his phone to call Aunt Phyllis, the police, and her insurance company—in that order—Charlie took another look at the car. If the driver side had taken the direct hit, she would've never walked away.

He swallowed against the lump in his throat and bent down to pick up a sippy cup that had been thrown out the broken window. What if Charlotte had been in the car?

Tears burned his eyes.

When he turned his head to survey the fender damage, he saw a beer can glistening in the setting sun. Stupid kids. He used to toss his empties out the window on this stretch of road, too. Now, he couldn't imagine being so careless.

He had way too much to lose.

Standing with the sippy cup in hand, he opened the back door to retrieve the booster seat and anything else Morgan might need before the car was towed. An unopened six-pack, sans one can, littered the floor behind the passenger seat.

Charlie balked. No way. Morgan wouldn't have been drinking and driving. She'd never been big on booze. And even if what Pamela said had driven her to drink, she couldn't have been drunk off one beer. But still … Maybe the comment about losing Charlotte was because of the beer.

No matter how much she did or didn't drink, it did look pretty bad. Some people would jump at the chance to persecute her for this.

He scooped up the six-pack and grabbed the stray can off the ground. Then, he tossed them onto the front seat of his truck. It was better if the police and tow truck driver didn't find them among the wreckage.

People were already jumping to too many conclusions where Morgan was concerned.

She stood with her back to him in the field beyond the car. Every once in a while she lifted her free hand toward her face, but then yanked it back down again.

He smiled. She was listening to him.

The biggest, fattest sense of peace and right washed him from head to toe. She was alive, and he was so fucking grateful.

He wanted her to know.

• • •

Morgan answered Officer Daly's questions despite the splitting headache and ringing in her ears. The paramedics had told her to go to the ER in Rileyville if things got worse. She just wanted to go to Aunt Phyllis's house, cuddle up with Charlotte, and forget this day ever happened.

"How fast were you going?" Office Daly asked.

"I don't remember." Which was a lie. She'd been going too fast, but she wasn't going to say that.

He scribbled something on his pad.

Charlie wrapped an arm around her shoulders and pulled her closer. "Can we hurry this up? She needs to rest."

Morgan relaxed against him, careful of her sore shoulder and the bruising on her face. She couldn't believe he was here, but she was so thankful he was.

"Of course." Officer Daley said. "Let me just have a few words with Jay before he tows the vehicle, and you can be on your way."

Alone again, Morgan rolled into Charlie, and he surrounded her with both arms. When she closed her eyes, images of the deer and then the tree, flashed in her head. She tensed.

He kissed the top of her head and smoothed his hands over her back. "It's almost over, and then I'll get you home to Charlotte."

She would've cried in relief if she wasn't so worried the tears would burn her wounds.

"Cramer, is this your truck?"

When Morgan looked up, Officer Daly was looking into the cab of Charlie's truck.

Charlie inhaled, and she rose up on his chest. "It is."

"You know it's against the law to have an open container in your vehicle?"

Morgan's heart stopped. She hadn't had a chance to talk to Charlie about what Alice said the other night. Was he really drinking again? "Charlie?"

He lifted a palm to halt her words. "It's not what you think." And then he called, "I wasn't drinking it" to the officer.

"Doesn't matter. That's an open container inside your vehicle. I'm going to have to cite you."

Charlie's growl rumbled through Morgan. "Fine, then cite me. Just let us get the hell out of here."

"I'll have to confiscate the alcohol."

"I don't care." Charlie tipped Morgan's chin and lowered his face. "I promise you I was not drinking."

No matter what Alice said or saw, Morgan believed him.

Officer Daly walked toward them with a ticket in hand and a six-pack tucked beneath his arm. She recognized the beer immediately. That was hers, left over from the picnic with Mark. She'd told him she'd take it, so Margaret wouldn't smell it or see it.

Her jaw dropped. Charlie must've thought *she'd* been drinking. He was trying to protect her.

Absolutely not! She wouldn't let him take the fall for her. "That's my beer. That's not his. I wasn't drinking it while I was driving, though. It's from a picnic weeks ago. I forgot it was in there."

Officer Daly furrowed his brow. "I don't know what's going on here, but I found the open container in Charlie's truck. The citation goes to him."

He reached toward Officer Daly for the ticket, but he looked at her. "Don't worry about it. I'm a big boy. I can handle the consequences of my actions."

She wanted to scream, but she knew it wouldn't do any good.

"Don't let this become a habit again, Charlie. Get some help." Officer Daly tipped his hat at Morgan. "I'll be in touch, Miss Parrish. Take it easy."

After that it was just Jay, hauling away the wreckage.

"I wish you hadn't done that," she said.

"Yeah, well, I thought I was protecting you. I didn't think it would come back to bite me like that." Charlie helped her into his truck, and then he climbed behind the wheel.

"People are going to think you're drinking again."

"If word gets out, probably. But do you think I'm drinking again?"

She shook her head. "No."

"Then that's what matters. I'll handle whatever comes of it." He reached for her hand. "Now, let's get you home to Charlotte."

Warmth from her palm climbed her arm and fanned across her body until she dropped her head to the seat and closed her eyes. He made everything better for her, while she made everything worse for him. Word would surely get around about the open container violation, and Alice wasn't going to be the only one who would rightfully blame her.

Rolling her head against the seat and opening her eyes, she looked at him again, ready to apologize. The muscle in his cheek pulsed, and her heart broke. "Charlie?"

He faced her, and for a second, shared her misery, but then he smiled and squeezed her hand. "I'm so fucking glad you're okay."

"Me, too."

She just wished there was a way they could be okay together. What he'd done today only further displayed the jeopardy she put him in by being here.

Chapter Thirteen

Charlie jolted awake at the sound of pounding on his front door. *What the hell?*

"Go away!" He rolled onto his stomach and slammed a pillow over his head.

Then he remembered what had happened yesterday. The scene at the restaurant. Morgan's crash. "His" open-container violation.

He'd bet everything he had that the pounding on his door had something to do with one of those things.

And he was right. Alice stood on his front porch with her blue eyes blazing and her hands on her hips.

"Were you drinking and driving?" She yanked open the screen door and shoved against his chest.

His blood pressure spiked. Why was she always thinking the worst about him? "I wasn't drinking, Alice." He swatted her hands away.

"Then why were you cited for an open-container violation? It's all over the mayor's office. Are you going to deny it?"

If he thought he could get away with it, yes. But he knew damn well when he'd accepted the citation that this town was going to have a field day with it.

He sank to the couch. "I'm not going to deny it. There was an open can of beer in my truck, and I was cited for it."

"Charlie," she wailed. "Why was there an open can of beer in your truck?"

"It wasn't mine."

"Whose was it?" Her eyes were going to pop out of her head if she didn't calm down. "It was hers!" She gasped. "Is that why she wrecked? People are saying there was a huge fight at the bistro, and you and Morgan ran off like Bonnie and Clyde."

"Holy shit, Alice. When did you start listening to what these people say? After all the crap they made up about you." He dropped his face to his hands.

"There are multiple eye-witness accounts of what happened at the bistro, and there's a police report detailing the accident. This is not just vicious gossip."

Too bad her precious eyewitness accounts and police report weren't telling the whole story. He grabbed a pillow, curled up on the couch, and closed his eyes. "I'm tired."

"You're throwing away everything for a woman who threw you away three years ago. You only own twenty percent of that bistro. Do you think for a minute the Mitchells are going to keep funding the rest if you're acting like this?"

"I don't know, Alice. You're a Mitchell. You tell me." Yeah, he was being a smart ass, but he couldn't help it. He really was too tired to deal with her.

"Charlie!" She punched his upper arm.

He groaned.

In the distance, his cell phone rang.

"You're just going to ignore that, too, aren't you?"

"Yep."

He heard her footsteps soften against the hardwood floors. And then, it was blessedly quiet except for the faint ringing.

"You should probably answer it," Alice said.

Oh, joy! She'd returned. Maybe if he didn't say anything, she'd go away again.

"It's Margaret."

Son of a bitch.

He answered his phone. The alternative was more guff from Alice. *That* was torture. Hopefully, Margaret's execution would be quick and painless.

No such luck. She wanted a meeting before she chopped off his head.

Fortunately, Will was in the meeting, too. He would be the voice of reason. Although, there wasn't much reasoning to be done. Charlie was guilty of almost everything he could be accused of. And what he wasn't guilty of, he wouldn't admit. Talk about being screwed.

Margaret leveled him with steely eyes. "Pamela Boardman is one of my oldest friends. She's also my bible study group leader."

Charlie lifted a brow. That wasn't saying much for Margaret's taste in friends or the state of her bible study. "I'm sorry." The words definitely held a double meaning.

She sniffed. "Your apology is insufficient. We are the majority owners of that business. What you do reflects on us."

And the company people kept reflected on them, too. Pamela Boardman was a bitch. But he probably shouldn't say it like that. "With all due respect, Pamela Boardman was rude."

"She was also a customer," Margaret snapped. "The customer is always right."

"Not when the customer is verbally abusing my wait staff. And before you blame this on Morgan, remember who hired her."

Margaret hmphed.

Will tapped his pen against the boardroom table. "I'm sure my mother would agree with me that abuse of any kind should not be tolerated. Nobody wants a hostile work environment. Mrs. Boardman deserved a reprimand and removal if she didn't heed a respectable warning. My issue is that you verbally told innocent customers to leave and left the restaurant while they were seated." Will shook his head. "You can't do that, Charlie, especially not when you're the only chef."

"Corbin is my sous chef. He cooked when I left."

"Corbin has been your waiter for months. When was the last time he cooked a meal for a patron beyond last night?"

He stirred the sauce a time or two. Charlie hid a cringe with the wipe of his palm. He wanted to argue that none of this was his fault, but he knew better. He'd been the one chasing Corbin from the kitchen and scaring waitresses away. If he hadn't done that in the first place, then he wouldn't have needed Morgan to stay.

Will sighed. "I don't know what's going on with you, Charlie, but you need to take a break. Get yourself together. Make sure you're healthy for a business commitment like this."

Disappointing the guy who'd had faith in him in the first place made everything worse.

Charlie tried to take a breath, but his lungs were dead weight. He hadn't felt this worthless and hopeless in years. "If I take a few days off, can I have a second chance?"

Margaret wrinkled her face when she looked at Will.

"I want to close the bistro for a couple weeks, so we can decide how to proceed," Will said. "You'll still get paid. Just give me fourteen quiet days. If we decide to reopen, maybe we'll even rebrand. After what happened, we need a fresh start. Best case scenario, we reopen stronger, wiser, and with the help you need to make that place a stable success."

They were shutting him down like they'd threatened to do. Two weeks without creating menus or cooking for someone else? That sucked. Everything in the fridge would go to waste. His vendors would be left without their weekly orders.

Ah, hell. Who was he kidding? Milk and eggs were the least of his worries.

In two weeks, he might have to face the fact he'd lost his biggest dream.

• • •

Seeing Charlie's truck amble up Aunt Phyllis's driveway lifted Morgan's spirits. Her aches and pains were worse the day after the wreck, and without a car, she felt trapped.

Not that she had any place to go even if she had a vehicle. She hadn't heard back from Johnson Berger or his human resource manager about a second interview. Her future was still up in the air, but at least she had a future.

One thing was for sure, she would never step foot in that bistro again. She'd already caused Charlie too much trouble by being there.

"Daddy's here." She carefully hoisted Charlotte to her hip and pushed out onto the porch.

"Daddy!" Charlotte yelled. "Hi, Daddy."

"Hey, baby girl." He smiled, but the expression didn't reach his eyes. "How are you?" When he looked at Morgan and asked the same, his forehead crinkled.

Something was wrong—really wrong. He wasn't just worried about her. Maybe he was taking serious heat for the open container violation.

That made her feel even worse.

"I'm fine," she said. "How are you?"

"I'll be fine."

"Which means you aren't fine now. Why? What happened?"

"Daddy." Charlotte reached for him.

Morgan transferred her into his arms, and for a split second, his eyes sparkled. He kissed Charlotte's fingertips, and rubbed noses with her, but all too soon, the sadness returned.

"Alice stopped by to tell me that everyone in the mayor's office thinks I'm a drunk again, and then Will Mitchell informed me they're closing the bistro at least for a couple weeks ... " his jaw clenched, "so I can get myself together."

"How can they do that? You're part owner, too."

"Twenty percent. That's a far cry from one hundred."

Morgan winced. She'd done this to him—ruined everything he'd been trying to build. His reputation. His restaurant. "Charlie, this is crazy. That wasn't your beer. I'm going to call everyone in town and tell them the truth."

"Don't. That won't change anything for me—people are always going to think I'm the drunk—but it might make things worse for you." He balanced Charlotte's bum on the porch railing, wrapped his arms around her waist, and rested his chin on her head. She giggled.

Morgan's frustration built. "Stop protecting me. It's ruining you."

He swung Charlotte around a few times, and then finally put her down. "I'd rather be ruined than see you treated the way Pamela Boardman treated you."

"Don't say that," she whispered.

Charlie sat on the front steps. "Why shouldn't I say it? It's true."

Morgan snatched a rock from Charlotte's hand before it made it into her mouth and replaced it with a plastic shovel. "Play with this, sweetie."

The screen door rattled, and Aunt Phyllis appeared. "I have peanut butter and jelly for Miss Charlotte. And fishy crackers."

Charlotte dropped her shovel and squealed her way into the house.

"Afternoon, Phyllis," Charlie said.

"Charlie." Aunt Phyllis smiled, and when he turned around, she gave Morgan a pointed look, the kind that said, "work this out."

After all, here was a man who would ruin himself for her.

"I don't know what to do. I want to make this better for you." Morgan sat beside him on the steps. "Most of the time I think the only way anything's going to get better is if I go. And I can't even seem to manage that."

He looked at her quizzically.

Morgan took a breath. "I had a phone interview for a job in Denver and I haven't heard back."

The sole of his boot slapped hard against the step. "Of course you did." He leaned forward with elbows on his knees, and then looked back at her. "You don't always have to run to make things better."

"I wish I could believe that were true. But, Charlie, the way I see it is you were doing great before I got here, and then I came and all hell broke loose. If I go, you'll be able to get the bistro back on track, Alice will stop bugging you about whether or not I've driven you to drink"—she blew out a breath; this part was harder—"and you can ask out someone nice … like Carrie."

"Carrie? Who told you about Carrie?"

"Corbin."

Charlie shook his head. "If I had enough help, I'd fire him." But he chuckled.

"No, you wouldn't."

"I wouldn't. And I wouldn't ask Carrie out, either. She's not my type."

The tattoo above his heart had made it pretty clear who was. But she wasn't going to stick around and screw up his life until it was as bad as hers was. He could move on if she left. He'd have to. "My point is, things will eventually go back to some semblance of normalcy when I'm gone."

"*Pfft*." He reached out, picked up a rock and tossed it in front of them. "Before you came, I was just a moody chef. Now, I'm a proud father. Your leaving won't change that."

She didn't want to change that. "Yep." She smiled. "You'll always be Charlotte's daddy."

"But from a distance?" The hard edge in his voice challenged her.

Morgan picked at the hem of her sweater. "We'll work it out, Charlie. For Charlotte. We'll find a way to stay close."

He looked so sad, but he didn't argue, and he didn't beg her to stay. Not that she wanted him to. She'd already turned him down too many times to warrant another shot.

Sliding closer to him, she rested her head on his upper back. "I'm sorry. For everything."

He sighed and sat up, wrapping an arm around her shoulders. "I'm not. All the bullshit in the world is worth one smile from that little girl."

It felt like heaven to have someone who thought the same as she did.

It felt like hell to know she'd have to say goodbye to him again.

• • •

A few minutes after midnight, there was a knock on the glass of Aunt Phyllis's patio door.

"What the … ?" Aunt Phyllis released the footrest on her recliner and grabbed a baseball bat from underneath the couch, where Morgan was sitting. So, there was no gun, but there was a bat.

Morgan jumped up, her heart throbbing in her throat. "Who is it?"

"Nothing but trouble at this hour." Aunt Phyllis crept into the kitchen. "Grab a knife from the drawer."

Morgan was alarmed too, but she rolled her eyes a little. "I don't think trouble would knock."

"You've got a baby sleeping in this house. Grab a knife, girl."

Shit. Maybe Aunt Phyllis had enemies. "I'd rather call the cops."

"They won't get here fast enough."

She grabbed a knife, but set it on the counter.

"Stay behind me." Aunt Phyllis approached the door and pulled back the very edge of the curtain. "Oh for crying out loud! It's your mother."

Morgan gaped. Her mother was here? Somehow that was a scarier prospect than an actual burglar. Harboring a fugitive was no joke.

"Are you going to let her in?" Morgan stepped back into the shadows of the kitchen, not sure how she wanted Aunt Phyllis to answer.

"I suppose I have to." Aunt Phyllis opened the door, but she blocked her sister's path. "What do *you* want?"

"Philly, please. I know I've been … Oh, everything is so wrong. I … Please, let me in. I need to see my daughter."

The fear vanished, and Morgan stepped into the light. "Mom?"

Her mother's eyes widened. "You're hurt. What happened?"

"Nothing. I'm fine. It was a minor car accident." There was far more discomfort associated with seeing her mother again.

"Heinrich told me where you were. I'm sorry. This is such a horrible mess, and I never meant for you to get caught up in it. I just … I don't know what I was thinking." She reached into her pocket and pulled out a white envelope. "Take this. It's yours."

"What is it?"

"It's money from your savings account." She brushed a palm over Morgan's cheek. "I haven't done right by you for many years, so take it, please. I have to go."

Morgan's lungs squeezed. So many questions needed answers if she was ever going to get to the bottom of what happened with her family.

She looked at the thick envelope. "Where are you going?"

"Don't worry about that."

"How can I not worry about it? My family is being arrested. My mother is sneaking around back doors in the middle of the night. This impacts me, too. *Where* are you going?"

"Away. And if you're smart, you'll do the same thing. Start over far away from here. You don't deserve to pay the price for what we've done."

Morgan closed her eyes, and told herself to breathe. "I can't believe you were an active participant. I can't believe I didn't know my parents were crooks. We were so good at pretending everything was perfect when it clearly wasn't. Why? For how long were involved?"

"Long enough to have known better."

"Then why didn't you say something or stop him?"

"Like you said, we were good at pretending. We had a life and an image to uphold. Those things don't come easy. At least they didn't to us."

The Parrishes were a joke. Maybe she should change Charlotte's last name to Cramer.

"Don't run, Mom. Talk to the investigators. Tell them what you know. Maybe they can cut you a deal. Running won't solve anything."

Morgan almost snorted at the words coming out of her mouth. Hadn't Charlie said practically the same thing to her?

"You sound like Heinrich."

"Listen to him, Mom. Listen to me. Turn yourself in."

Her mother frowned as she turned to Aunt Phyllis. "I'm sorry, Philly. So, so sorry. You were always the better woman. Thank you for helping my baby … and her baby." Her voice broke. "Take good care of them."

Aunt Phyllis gave a crisp nod.

After her mother left, Morgan sank to the floor. That was as close to loving as she'd ever seen her mother be. How frustrating to think when they finally had an emotionally honest break in their relationship, they weren't free to build on it. Still, her mother had come back—with the money. The most selfish woman Morgan knew had thought of someone other than herself.

As she let that sink in, she thumbed through the stack of bills. Her pulse quickened. She'd never seen so much money in one place. Twenty-five thousand dollars—if it was all here. More than enough for first and last month's rent in a place where no one knew her. She could start over, and Charlie could start over, too.

Finally something was working out in her favor.

Chapter Fourteen

One more coat of blue paint, and the ceiling in Charlotte's bedroom would be ready for some clouds. Charlie stood back and admired his work with a smile on his face. It was the first crack in his shitty mood since before Morgan's accident.

Maybe it was a sign he was going to be okay. He hoped so, because the longer the funk lasted, the more he thought about taking a drink.

With his hand strangling the extension pole, he did some deep breathing. It didn't kill the thought of whiskey, but it dulled the ache. As long as he only *thought* about drinking, he'd be okay.

Charlie rested the pole on the edge of the paint pan and headed to the kitchen for some coffee.

"Hey."

Even with the windows open, he hadn't heard a car pull into the driveway or his brother-in-law's footsteps on the front porch. But there stood Justin, the mayor of Harmony Falls, the man who had been Charlie's best friend until the drinking and bad behavior became too big a liability for a future politician.

"Hey. The door's open." Charlie continued onto the kitchen.

"How's it going?"

He refused to look at him and dug in the pantry for coffee beans instead. "Well, that depends on why you're here. Either you're here because my sister sent you, or you're here because of what's being said in the mayor's office. Either way, how do you think I am?"

"Listen, all I really care about is that you're sober."

He latched onto the coffee bag and faced Justin. "If I tell you I'm sober, will you believe me?" The doubt was in Alice's eyes every time they were in the same room, and he was tired of it. He didn't need to see it in Justin's eyes, too. "For the rest of my life, anytime I screw up, people are going to automatically think it's because of booze. That sucks! But I'm sober, Justin. It's up to you whether or not you believe me."

The coffee grinder killed the conversation, but the racket sounded good to Charlie.

When it finally quieted, Justin said, "I believe you."

He relaxed a bit. Maybe it was stupid to trust the word of a career politician, but he wanted to. "Coffee?"

"Sounds good."

Justin sat at the breakfast bar, while Charlie moved around the kitchen, gathering cups, spoons, and cream.

"I heard Morgan is pretty banged up from the accident."

Talking about booze with Justin wasn't bad enough; they had to talk about Morgan, too. "It's minor stuff. She's good."

"She's lucky."

You're telling me. Charlie couldn't stop picturing the wreckage.

"She's lucky you were there," Justin added.

"Is that your tactful way of asking why I was there? Is that something *you* want to know, or something my sister has sent you to find out?"

Justin sighed. "You can drop the attitude, Charlie. There's no conspiracy here. I came because I thought you might need someone to talk to, like a … friend or a brother. I'm both, you know?"

Charlie nodded. He knew Justin longer and better than he knew anyone else—besides Alice. And Justin was a hell of a lot calmer than his drama queen sister. "I appreciate that."

"Morgan's never going to be the easiest topic of conversation between us. I pursued her when I knew you still had feelings for her, and you got me back good the night of her bachelorette party." He winced. "But some way, somehow, we have to find a way to get past all that. I love your sister, and I assume you love your little girl. What I'm not clear on are your feelings for Morgan."

Charlie watched the tar-like coffee puddle in the glass pot.

"What do you want to happen with her?"

Charlie's nose twitched. He didn't want to talk about this even though he'd been thinking a lot about it. He wanted to be with her. Hell, he'd even been fantasizing about giving up his dream about having a successful restaurant in Harmony Falls so he could follow her again.

"If you tell me, then maybe it will help us figure the rest out. Maybe I can help you reach your goals and find your happiness. I'm really good with planning. Ask your sister."

Alice would kill them both if she knew Charlie wanted to be with Morgan and Justin could possibly have anything to do with making that happen. "This is a waste of time. What I want is never going to happen." Because what he really wanted was his restaurant and Morgan, too.

"Come on, Charlie. Anything is possible."

Said Harmony Falls' golden boy. "Not when the odds have been stacked against you since birth, Mr. Mayor."

"I don't know. From where I'm sitting, I think you've accomplished some pretty big things against those odds. You got sober. You convinced my family to invest in a bistro instead of a bakery. And you have Charlotte. If you ask me, there's not much more a man could want … " Justin shot him a shrewd stare. "Unless you want the mother of your child, too."

That's exactly what he wanted. He roughed his hands over his face and nodded. "I'd take that."

"Then you need to tell her you love her, and you want to be with her. This turmoil will die down. God knows it died down for me and Alice. We managed. You and Morgan will manage, too."

The tiniest jolt of hope shocked Charlie's system. Could it really happen like that? Would the majority of people ever stop hating her enough for her to feel comfortable here with him? *A simple life with a simple man.*

Charlie turned his back on Justin and reached for the full pot. "It's a nice thought, but it's not going to work. She wants and deserves to live someplace where people aren't constantly judging her based on her mistakes and her last name. Charlotte deserves a better life than that, too."

"There's another option. You could go with them."

He shrugged. "I've thought of that, but I'd be walking away from the restaurant."

"You can cook anywhere. And someday, you'll open your own restaurant again. Only then, you'll own it outright, which means you won't have my mother looking over your shoulder. Bonus." He laughed. "Instead, you'll have Charlotte—and I'm betting Morgan, if you want her."

A couple months ago, that bistro was all he had, but now, he had more—including a little girl. This time, following Morgan just might work.

•••

Charlie's invitation for Morgan and Charlotte to have dinner at his house came out of the blue. Morgan was glad he called, because she wanted him to spend as much time as possible with Charlotte—especially now that she'd decided she was leaving.

Johnson Berger had finally called to set up an in-person interview for the corporate attorney position next week. With the money from her mother re-deposited in her account, she had enough to relocate now. Even if she didn't end up hired, Denver was as good a place as any.

At least that was what she kept telling herself.

Hopefully, the envelope she had stuffed in Charlotte's diaper bag would soften the blow to Charlie.

She stood on Aunt Phyllis's porch, watching his truck make the rocky climb up the gravel drive. It wasn't convenient for him to pick them up, but a replacement for her totaled car was dependent on an insurance check—which was taking way too long to arrive. She was going to have to rent a car to drive to Pittsburgh so she could fly to Denver. *Ugh.* She didn't know what she dreaded the more: the two-hour drive when she was still hesitant to get behind the wheel or leaving Charlotte for a couple days.

"Don't hurry back on my account." Aunt Phyllis stood behind the screen door. That woman was still trying to convince her that Charlie was the right man.

Morgan didn't need convincing. That would only make it harder to leave him.

She smiled and waved as she hauled Charlotte toward the truck.

"Afternoon, Phyllis." Charlie hopped down from the driver's side. Without being asked to, he sauntered to the porch and grabbed the booster seat. "Am I going to need a manual for this?"

Sunlight kissed the ends of his hair and brightened his eyes. God, he looked so happy—despite everything. What would he look like after she told him she and Charlotte were leaving?

Ugh.

She ignored the question. "It's not hard to install. Here, take the girlie. I'll do it. You can watch."

He grinned.

Ten minutes later, they were on their way. The town was hopping. Not a single open parking spot remained, and the line outside Alice's theater stretched to the end of the block.

"What's going on?" Morgan asked.

"Some kids' show."

Charlotte sat in the booster seat beside her, flipping through a picture book. Her feet bounced in time with the country music spilling from Charlie's radio. Someday, Morgan was going to take her to shows like that.

They passed the darkened bistro, and Charlie didn't even turn his head.

"Do you miss it, or are you enjoying the break?"

"I'm good—real good." He unleashed that smile again.

Guilt swelled. She grabbed onto Charlotte's hand and looked out the passenger window until they reached his house. The place had drastically changed since she'd been there three years ago hurling insults at Alice on the front porch.

"You painted." The siding used to be dingy white. Now, it was a pristine bluish-gray.

"Yep."

"You landscaped, too."

He stood beside her with Charlotte on his hip. "Without Alice's dog around digging them up, I can have a vegetable garden again."

"Me see gog?" Charlotte yelped. She swiveled around in Charlie's arms, looking for an animal.

"No, dog, here, babe."

Charlie stopped on the porch. Probably to get his keys from his pocket and unlock the door. But then he faced Morgan. "Do you remember the last time we stood here?"

This had been the exact spot they'd been standing in when she'd told him she was pregnant less than a week after Justin called off the wedding. She nodded. "I do." She rubbed a hand over Charlotte's bare leg, barely able to imagine a life without her daughter. "I like how things turned out. It's much better than what I'd proposed that day."

"Much." He kissed Charlotte on the forehead and then opened the front door.

The interior of the house had changed, too. "You put in hardwood floors."

"They were underneath all that gross carpet." He set Charlotte down, and in a blink, she was off to explore. Morgan hoped he'd thought to baby proof the place.

Following her to make sure afforded Morgan a look at more of the improvements. The kitchen, especially, was amazing. Fitting for a chef.

She smiled at Charlie as she scrambled down the hallway after Charlotte. "You do good work."

"Thanks."

Something in the room at the end of the hall grabbed Charlotte's attention. "Hey, you little monkey. What are you doing in … ?" Morgan stilled in the doorway.

Charlotte sat in the middle of plush green carpet with a pile of scattered building blocks and other toys around her. A twin bed was tucked in the corner, and sunny yellow walls stretched to meet a pale blue ceiling. A room. For Charlotte. And she wasn't even going to get the chance to use it.

Her guilt multiplied.

"It's not done." Charlie's hand gripped her left shoulder and squeezed.

"You did this for her?"

"I wanted her to wake up to a sunny day even when it was snowing or raining."

Morgan's head drooped. She couldn't prolong this anymore. "Charlie, we're leaving."

"I know that."

"I mean, we're leaving soon. I'm going to interview for that job in Denver, and while I'm there, I'm going to find a place to live."

"Okay."

God, he was taking this awfully well. His cool only ramped up her anxiety. "What do you mean okay? You did all this work. You were hoping we would stay, weren't you?"

"I did all this work ... before I decided to go with you." He smiled as his glance shifted from her to Charlotte. "If you're moving to Denver, then I'm moving to Denver, too."

Morgan's knees weakened, and she reached for the doorjamb behind her. "What? I mean why? How ... "

Charlie cupped her face. "I love you. I've always loved you. That's why I got these." He tapped his chest. "The day I got the paternity papers, when I thought I'd lost you for good, I walked in and had both dates carved over my heart. I don't care what it takes. I'm not going to lose you or Charlotte again."

"But the bistro ... "

"I think there are bistros in Denver."

Charlotte's voice grew louder. "Dad. Dad! Daddy! Build wit me."

Charlie pressed a soft kiss to Morgan's lips and went to join his daughter.

She stood in the doorway, admiring them. Could she really have a life like this? Was she entitled to it, if it came as the result of Charlie walking away from his restaurant ... his house ... and his sister?

"Mama," Charlotte yelled. "Build wit me."

"I'm coming, baby girl." She sank to the floor beside them.

It did feel awfully good to be a family.

She laid one hand on Charlie's thigh and the other on Charlotte's. "I want this. I want us." She looked into his beautiful eyes. "I love you, too."

That's when she remembered the papers in the diaper bag. "Wait right here."

When she returned, she placed the envelope in his lap.

"What's this?"

"Open it. You'll see."

He scanned the copy of Charlotte's birth certificate and glanced at the paper underneath it. "I don't understand."

"She's Charlotte Parrish on there. She's Charlotte Cramer in here." Morgan pointed to her heart, and then to Charlie's. "These papers will change that."

He blinked more than necessary and sniffed a few times, too. "Are you sure?"

There was still a lot she wasn't sure of, but changing Charlotte's surname wasn't on the list. "Absolutely."

At least one of them should have a last name she could be proud of.

• • •

After they played, they ate, and then Charlotte fell asleep. Charlie carried her to bed, leaving Morgan on the couch with her legs curled beneath her.

She absorbed the quiet. This had been the most peaceful, perfect evening of her entire life.

And he was coming to Denver with her, where they could work toward a lifetime of nights like this. It was more than she ever would have hoped.

So why did a kernel of doubt niggle in her brain?

Eventually, Charlie returned to the living room with ginger ale in frosted mugs and two pieces of chocolate cake. "Rumor has it this is the best dessert in Harmony Falls."

Her heart pinched. Hopefully, it would become the best dessert in Denver, too. "Well, if you made it, then I believe it."

"Don't you want to taste it first?" He handed her a plate and sat beside her, his thigh brushing hers.

The warmth and closeness assuaged her doubt.

"What do you think?" he asked.

She sighed as chocolate melted on her tongue. "I think you're amazing."

He bobbed his brows. "In *and* out of the kitchen."

Very true. She smiled, but then the thought of him being completely out of the kitchen stole her glee. "What if you can't find a chef position in Denver? Or what if you end up cooking someplace where you can't make chocolate cake?" Maybe it sounded silly, but she was serious.

"Then I'll make it for you and Charlotte at home."

Which would be wonderful. But she could only eat so much chocolate cake. And he could only be happy cooking for the three of them so long. He was more than that. "You need to be cooking for lots of people in your own restaurant, where you can decide the menu. Are you going to be able to find that in Denver?"

"Maybe I can find a job in a restaurant that hasn't opened yet, get in on the ground floor and help shape it. And if not, well, it'll be my goal to own a place again someday. I'll just have to work for it even harder this time."

How long would that take? She didn't want him to have to wait because of her. "What if I invested twenty thousand dollars? Would that be enough to get started?"

His brows lifted. "I thought you were broke."

"I was. Until my mother showed up with the twenty-five thousand she took from my savings account. Insurance is paying to replace my totaled car, so that's a wash, and this Denver job comes with a moving allowance. Surely I can get by on the remaining five thousand plus what I've saved working for you until I get my first paycheck. What can you do with twenty thousand dollars?"

"A lot. But, I can't take your money. I'm sure you had plans for it."

"Well, sure. If I don't get this job, then we'll need the money to get by until I find another one."

"You don't think you'll get this one?"

She shook her head. "I don't know. Honestly, I don't even know if I want it. If it's offered to me, I'll take it, of course, but I don't want to be a corporate attorney anymore." Then again, life hadn't been about what she wanted since she laid eyes on Charlotte.

"What do you want to be?"

"A good mom to Charlotte. Other than that, I want to do something dynamic where every day is different, and I'm busy, but having fun."

"With spreadsheets and conversation?" He grinned.

"Exactly. Hey, maybe I don't need to spend the rest of my life practicing law. Once you're up and running and we're stable, you could hire me to manage your new restaurant. I can hire, fire, order, and keep things running smoothly … so *you* can just cook."

He squeezed her thigh. "I like the sound of that. And, you know what? Once I sell this house, we'll have even more money. It should be enough to get us a place just like Char-Grilled Bistro in Denver." He leaned back on the couch and widened his legs, the picture of calm amidst the dramatic conversation.

It seemed a little silly for them to spend all this money just to recreate the life they'd had.

She set her plate on the end table. "Are you sure about this? What are the Mitchells going to do if you leave and they decide to reopen the bistro? And Alice is going to freak."

He smoothed a hand along her arm. "Corbin can cook. They'll probably have an easier time staffing the place with him in charge." His smile twisted a bit, but didn't fade. "And Alice will survive. She has her theater and her husband to keep her happy. I deserve someone to keep me happy, too." He wrapped his hand around her upper arm and tugged. "Now come here, so I can show you just how sure I am."

Chapter Fifteen

Charlie planted a trail of kisses up Morgan's belly to her ear. "You taste better than my chocolate cake."

"Then I must taste pretty damn good."

He smiled as he caressed the soft curves of her body and dipped his fingers between her legs where his mouth had been. "So good I'd rather have you than chocolate cake any day." Every day. That's why he was going to follow her away from Harmony Falls—again.

Dropping his open mouth over the tight skin of her collarbone, he traced her with his tongue. He'd always preferred salty over sweet.

She rocked her hips against his erection, and he groaned. A second later, he slid inside of her for release.

He'd made love to this woman dozens of frantic, sweaty, desperate times, but never like this. Soft and slow. Effortless. Intimate. Just two people in love—with a future *together*.

Yeah, he wanted this. Giving up everything for her was the right thing to do.

The intensity built between them until she wrapped her legs around him and urged him deeper. He thrust harder. Harder still.

She slid her hands to his face and brought them nose to nose, eye to eye. "I love you."

Hearing her say those words was the icing on the cake.

When they'd finished and dressed, he followed her down the hallway to check on Charlotte. The nightlight he'd found in a junk drawer kept her company in her new bed. At least she got to use the room once. *No regrets.*

Still, his chest tightened.

Morgan kissed him under the chin. "Maybe she could stay here with you while I'm interviewing."

Charlie nodded. He'd like that. Seeing her here made him realize what a great house this was for a family. Somebody was bound to buy it fast. Again, his chest tightened. *No regrets.*

He could buy a new home for his family—in Denver.

"Maybe we should just stay here," she said.

His heart swelled.

"You know? Instead of you driving us back to Aunt Phyllis's tonight, maybe we could spend the night."

It surprised him how relieved he'd felt when he'd thought she'd been talking about staying in Harmony Falls. After all the shit that had happened here, he'd have thought leaving would be as much of a relief for him as it was going to be for her. But he'd accomplished a lot in this town over the last couple of years. The idea of starting over somewhere else was daunting … and depressing.

"Is it okay if we stay?" She wrapped her arms around his waist.

"Of course, it is. In fact … you should move in here until we leave."

Might as well get some use out of the place. Maybe that would help him feel more excited about the move.

The next morning, Charlie woke early and made pancakes that Charlotte nearly inhaled. His smile lingered. Watching his kid devour something he made was a pretty big rush. Having the kid's mother kiss the cook while he was refilling orange juice was even better.

He was going to make every morning like this.

After breakfast, he found Morgan standing at the kitchen sink, looking out over the backyard.

"It's such a pretty yard, Charlie. So wide, and green, and peaceful. It just goes on and on. My house in town had this little postage stamp of green between the pool house and the pool, and the entire thing was closed off by wrought iron. I'd always felt so trapped." She spun around to face him. "My condo in Connecticut wasn't any better. It was surrounded by pavement.

You know, Charlotte never played on grass until we came to Aunt Phyllis's?" She shook her head. "That sucks. Kids need to run."

"Agreed." He nuzzled her neck.

"Denver will have spaces like this, right?"

"I think so."

"Good. Because when I'm there, I'm going to look for a house just like this."

If he didn't know how badly she wanted out of Harmony Falls, he might have thought she was having second thoughts, too.

When they were all loaded in the truck and heading back to Phyllis's, Morgan looked at him. "I'm going to miss Aunt Phyllis. I wish I could convince her to go with us."

He smiled. "I don't think there's a U-Haul big enough for all those cats and chickens."

"Still, if I could tear her away from that place. I would." She propped her elbow on the door and stared out the window.

This was not the Morgan Parrish who left Harmony Falls three years ago. That woman worried more about toeing her family's line than she did other people's feelings. He reached over Charlotte's booster seat, tickling her knee as he passed, and then he latched onto Morgan's hand. "Maybe I can convince her to go with us."

She smiled and squeezed his hand. "She does like your boots."

The minute they saw the gleaming black Escalade parked in front of Phyllis's house, the easy moment died.

"Shoot." Morgan looked at Charlotte and then at him. "That doesn't look good. Government plates. Maybe they found my mom. We gave her a head start, but then Aunt Phyllis called the police."

He parked far enough back so that the SUV could turn around to exit. Hopefully, they'd be leaving soon. But just in case … "I'm going in with you."

"You don't have to do that."

"Yes, I do. You don't know what you're walking into."

•••

With shoulders back and chin lifted, Morgan entered the house. "Hello?"

"In the kitchen," Aunt Phyllis said.

For some reason, the tone of Aunt Phyllis's voice had Morgan passing Charlotte off to Charlie. "Maybe you should take her into another room and keep her busy."

"Yep … as soon as I make sure everything is okay in that kitchen."

Morgan planted a quick kiss to his cheek. His support kept her from jumping out of her skin.

Aunt Phyllis was sitting at the kitchen table with two men in dark suits. They stood when they saw Morgan.

"Miss Parrish, I'm Agent Clarke, and this is Agent Gorman."

They flashed badges as they scrutinized Charlie.

Morgan reached forward for handshakes. "Nice to meet you. This is my … daughter, Charlotte, and her father, Charlie Cramer."

The men nodded when Charlie said hello.

"Miss Parrish, we have a few questions for you about your mother."

Charlotte started to cry.

"Go ahead and take her in the other room or outside to play," Morgan said. "I'll be fine."

Charlie gave the agents a very pointed look. "I'll be right outside." It was silly but touching.

Charlie and Charlotte went out the back door, and the agents returned to their chairs.

"We've been talking to your aunt about your mother," Agent Clarke said.

"Were you surprised to see her?"

Aunt Phyllis circled the table refilling the agents' coffee cups.

"I was absolutely floored to see my mother." Otherwise she never would've let Aunt Phyllis talk her into taking that knife out of the drawer.

"Was anyone else with her?"

"Not that I could see. I never heard a car pull up, and I didn't think to look for one after she left." After she'd picked herself up off the floor, she'd gone straight to bed to cuddle with Charlotte, while Aunt Phyllis called the local police.

"Do you have any idea where she might've gone, after she stopped here? Any sympathetic friends in the area or surrounding states?"

Heinrich. But she couldn't imagine outing the man who'd been so nice to her when she'd first arrived in town. Besides, he was trying to get her mother to do the right thing. "She said she was going away. That's it. I couldn't begin to guess where. She and I have had a very strained and separate relationship for the last three years."

"Then why do you think she would risk coming here?"

"I have no idea," Aunt Phyllis said, before she could answer. "The woman's crazy!"

"When was the last time you saw your sister before she showed up?"

"More than 30 years ago … when she married the man I loved."

Morgan's jaw dropped. Aunt Phyllis had been in love with Dad?

"And, you, Miss Parrish? When was the last time you saw your mother before she came here?"

"A little over a year ago … on my daughter's first birthday." The words sort of spilled out while Morgan stared at Aunt Phyllis. *She'd been in love with Dad?*

Agent Gorman cleared his throat. "Why do you think she came here out of the blue?"

Think? Morgan knew. And there was no use trying to cover up the truth, unless Morgan wanted to become more embroiled in this investigation than she had to. "My mother withdrew several thousand dollars from a joint account that was set up for me when I was a child. It was the culmination of some hefty savings bonds and then years of monetary gifts for birthdays, first communion, graduation—that sort of thing. It had been my intention to keep it for my daughter's college education, but then I needed it, and that's when I realized it was gone. She must've felt guilty about taking it, because she brought it back to me."

The agents exchanged looks.

"We'll need access to that account, Miss Parrish."

Morgan nodded. Of course they would. The minute her mother touched the credit union account, the assets were destined to be tied up, too. On some level, Morgan had known that. She'd just been so caught up in the hope and freedom the money represented.

She could file a motion to have the money released, but she had no idea how long that would take. One thing she did know: without that twenty-five-thousand dollars, the plans she and Charlie made last night were hollow.

Once the agents left and Charlotte was napping, Morgan filled Charlie in on what had happened. He took the financial loss better than Morgan had.

"I can cook anywhere," he said again.

But she didn't want him cooking someone else's food in someone else's kitchen. This was not helping to quiet her second thoughts.

He left an hour later.

Morgan pulled the curtains away from the front window and watched his truck disappear down the driveway. Was life ever going to be easy for them?

"You shouldn't have said anything about the money." Aunt Phyllis sat on the recliner, brushing mats from a cat that was sprawled on her lap.

"I'm a lawyer. I know what kind of trouble I could get into withholding something like that from an investigation."

Aunt Phyllis shrugged. "Sometimes you need to take risks in order to keep the man you love."

True, but no woman needed to be doing anything illegal to keep a man. That was crazy. And *this* was probably not about Morgan and Charlie. "*You* were in love with my father?"

She huffed. "Ancient history."

"It didn't seem so ancient this afternoon when you told those agents. I saw your face, Aunt Phyllis. You looked upset. What happened?"

Her eyes sort of glazed over as her strokes lengthened on the cat. "Once upon a time there were two very young and pretty Marion girls, but they were different as night and day. Kitty was tall and thin and poised. Philly was short and plump and silly. One day, a young man moved into town with his family. The Parrishes." She smiled. "They were from a bigger city back East, and they had style like nobody in these parts had ever seen. Robert Parrish was just as poised as Kitty, and on paper, they made a perfect match. But, Robert liked to laugh, and he found he could laugh with Philly. That laughter turned to love." Her smile dropped. "Only, it couldn't last, because Robert and Kitty were declared the perfect couple everywhere they turned. They had their parents' blessings, too. And when it came time to ask for somebody's hand, Robert chose Kitty."

How awful! Bits of the story replayed in her head, mixing with scenes from her own manipulated engagement to Justin. It was bad enough the ridiculous happened once; it happened again decades later when they should've known better.

She hugged Aunt Phyllis. "I'm so sorry."

"I'm not." She patted Morgan's arm. "Not anymore. Certainly not now that he's in prison."

"I can't believe I never heard that story before."

"Who would've told you? Not your parents. And this town didn't know the half of it. Robert and I did a lot of sneaking around."

Like Morgan and Charlie had done.

"I should've known then that there was no future for a relationship that couldn't be carried on in public. And that man, he asked everything of me, and I gave it. Real love, the kind that lasts, takes equal sacrifices."

Morgan collapsed on the couch amid a swirl of sickening recognition. She was asking Charlie to do a lot of those same things. He was giving up everything: his bistro, his house, his family and friends. What was she sacrificing? What had she ever sacrificed for him?

"Oh my God." She covered her mouth. "I can't make him leave, and I love him too much to leave without him. I have to stay."

Aunt Phyllis smiled. "It's about damn time you figured that out."

Morgan laughed. No matter where she went, there would always be someone who didn't like her. But only here in Harmony Falls could she count on three people to love her unconditionally.

She jumped off the couch and planted a kiss to Aunt Phyllis's cheek. "Thank you for helping me see this. I love you."

Aunt Phyllis squeezed her wrist. "And I love you. You know, the worst part of losing Robert was losing the dreams I had of being a mother to his children. Funny how life works, isn't it?"

Morgan kissed her again.

"Now git." Aunt Phyllis swatted her away. "Take my beast of a car. She ain't pretty but she should run. I'll watch baby girl while you go tell that man he doesn't have to sell his house, because you're staying."

Morgan smiled. She was going to do better than that.

There was a bistro bearing Charlie's name that needed to be re-opened, staffed, and booked. And she knew just the people who could make that happen.

Chapter Sixteen

Before Morgan could meet with the Mitchells, she had someone else to see. This meeting was going to be the toughest. But, in the spirit of sacrifice, compromise, and all that was holy in healthy relationships, she dug her heels in and readied for the storm.

Alice wrapped her hands around a can of cola as she sat on a stool at her kitchen counter. "Why do I get the feeling I'm not going to like what I'm about to hear?"

"Because you're not going to like the first part. Keep in mind it does get better, though."

She gave a dramatic sigh and rolled her eyes. "Then let's get it over with."

Morgan dropped her feet to the floor and slipped off the stool. She needed to pace for this. "I know why Charlie is coming over here later tonight. He's going to tell you he's selling the house and moving to Denver with me and Charlotte."

"What!" Alice slapped her hands against the counter.

"Remember, it gets better."

"I hope so."

Morgan took a deep breath. "He's going to tell you those things, but I'm not going to let him do those things. I love him, and I've decided to stay in Harmony Falls, so we can be together."

"I thought you said this gets better." Alice sneered.

"You want your brother to be happy, don't you?"

"Of course, I do. I want him happy, but I want him to be sober, too."

"Alice, he is sober! He's so sober it isn't funny. Everything that has happened since I've been here, and he hasn't taken a single drink."

"He almost did."

"Almost doesn't count. Either you drink, or you don't, and he didn't. He's not your father. He's not going to end up like him. And I'm not my father—or my mother. I'm not going to make the same mistakes they've made. I want a simple, happy life for my daughter. I also want Charlie. Will you help me?"

"You want *me* to help *you* have Charlie?"

"Ironic, isn't it?"

Alice crossed her arms and narrowed her eyes. "What do you need me to do?"

"When he comes over tonight, I need you to give him your blessing to sell the house and leave town with me. Don't fight him. Don't tell him you talked to me."

"Why not? You said you weren't going to make him do those things."

"I'm not, but I don't want him to know that yet. I have a meeting with the Mitchells after this. I'm going to get the bistro re-opened. I want to have everything in place before I tell him we're staying. I want him to see how serious I am. He was willing to give up everything to be with me—twice. I want to make sure he doesn't have to give up anything ever again. From now on, if anyone needs to sacrifice, it's me."

Alice's perfectly arched eyebrows rose and Morgan held her breath as Charlie's sister regarded her with exacting scrutiny.

"Well, amen," she finally said, and then she smiled.

It was the first time Alice had smiled at her in years.

With one meeting down, Morgan headed confidently into the next. But her palms began to sweat and her mouth went dry the minute she faced all four Mitchells. "Thank you for meeting with me on such short notice."

Margaret and Justin glanced at Mark. No doubt he played a big part in getting them here.

Will, on the other hand, looked truly interested in whatever she had to say. His brows lifted high on his head. "What can we do for you?"

Again, Morgan forewent the chair. She paced the length of the boardroom table, trying to stabilize her heart rate. "I want you to reopen the bistro with Charlie as chef and Corbin as sous chef. I know you told him you wanted time and for him to get himself together … " she drew air-quotes around the words, "but I can assure you that's not necessary. The beer he was cited for was mine. He was protecting me and our daughter when he grabbed it out of my car and put it in his. Charlie is a good man and a good cook, and he deserves your respect and that restaurant. Everything he has is wrapped up in that dream, but he's willing to leave town with me, so we can raise Charlotte together. That's the kind of person he is. That's the kind of person I want to be. So I'm staying here in Harmony Falls with him—as long as he has your full support."

"*You* were drinking and driving?" Margaret asked.

Morgan sighed. "This isn't about me, but no. I wasn't. That beer was left over from a picnic that didn't include Charlie."

Mark cleared his throat. "I can vouch for that. Actually, I can do better than that. The beer was mine."

Margaret's eyes bulged. "You don't drink beer."

"I do." Mark said. "Just not around you, because I know how much you hate it."

Justin shook his head, and Will hid a laugh behind his hand.

"Forget about the beer," Justin said. "This is about the bistro."

Will nodded. "I'm okay with reopening. Charlie has my support. He always has."

Justin and Mark agreed.

Margaret stared at something over the top of Morgan's head. "Well, considering I'm the one who pushed you to waitress there in the first place, which wasn't such a good idea, I suppose it's only right to give him another chance."

"Why did you push me there?" Morgan asked.

Justin raised his hand. "Let me answer this one. You knew it would bring people through the door didn't you, Mother?"

"I thought it might cause a much-needed buzz about the restaurant, yes."

Morgan frowned. She'd been a corporate sacrifice for her father, and now Margaret? Well, never again. "Just so we're clear, I won't be waitressing at the bistro when it reopens." Margaret nodded. "I'll be managing it. Charlie needs someone behind the scenes, dealing with the vendors and employees, so he can just cook."

Margaret huffed. "Well, I don't know how that's going to work. What will people think after everything that's happened?"

"I don't care what people think." Morgan smiled. It felt good to say those words and really mean them for the first time in her life. She'd learned that sort of gutsiness from Charlie. "This time, we're going to put everything we have into making that place a success, and we're going to do it together. That's all I care about."

"I think that's great," Justin said.

"And another thing." This was the big one. "Before the bistro re-opens, I want it in writing that Charlie can buy you out as soon as he has the capital. I have twenty-five thousand dollars coming my way at some point, and I'll be adding that to the twenty percent he already holds."

Margaret gasped, Justin nodded, and Mark grinned.

"I think that's reasonable," Will said.

"Good." This was easier than she'd thought it would be. Funny what happened when she was guided by love and not by fear. "Thank you. Now, one last thing…"

"Oh, for crying out loud," Margaret said.

Morgan smiled. "What are the chances you could reopen the bistro tomorrow or the next night?"

"Slim to none. Right, William?"

"Well, I don't know. What's the rush?" he asked.

"That's where I'd like to ask Charlie to marry me."

•••

Charlie stared at the woman leaning against the refrigerator in Alice and Justin's kitchen. She looked like Alice. She sounded like Alice. But, she had to be an imposter. His sister would've never taken this announcement so gracefully. "Did you hear what I said?"

She nodded. "Yep. I sure did."

"And you're not mad that I'm selling the house and moving to Denver."

"Nope."

"What about Morgan?"

"What about her?"

"She's the reason I'm doing this."

Alice lifted one shoulder and scrunched up her face. "I can't worry about that anymore. I have Justin and my theater. I'm happy. I want you to be happy, too. If you're telling me selling the house and running off with Morgan will make you happy, then who am I to stop you?"

Huh. Charlie crossed his arms over his chest. She was being so damn mature about this. Maybe their last conversation finally sunk in. "You're not worried about me drinking anymore?"

She shook her head. "I've always wanted to believe you were sober. I was just so scared that if I believed it, I'd let my guard down, and I wouldn't be able to help you if you needed me to. I'm tired of being afraid, Charlie."

Now that? *That* was his honest, sincere sister. "Thank you."

She dabbed beneath her shiny eyes.

"Wow. I'm floored by how cool you're being. Are you going to be this nice to Morgan when you see her again?"

"Of course." But her expression tightened just a bit.

Gotcha! He bit back a laugh. "That's awesome. She'll be so happy to hear it. We were worried we wouldn't have any place to stay when we came back to town for holidays. Now, we can just stay here."

She opened her mouth, but snapped it shut a second later.

"You're up to something," he said.

"Never."

"Alice Cramer, you've been up to something since the day you were born."

She cackled. "You're paranoid. Get out of here, Charlie, before I change my mind and have the mayor invoke eminent domain over that house so you can't move." She lifted her chin real snooty like. "I know the mayor, and he would totally do that for me."

Yeah. He knew the mayor, too, and that guy was definitely a sucker for melodramatic blondes.

The next day, when Charlie told Morgan about Alice's reaction, her reaction was just as strange.

"That's great." She reached into his refrigerator and poured Charlotte a cup of milk.

Charlie's brows shifted. It *was* great, but … "That's all you have to say? Don't you wonder why she isn't more upset?"

"Don't go borrowing trouble, Charlie. Let's just be happy things are looking good and moving along."

Maybe she was just trying to stay extra optimistic in preparation for Tuesday's interview. "What if I went with you on Tuesday?"

"Where?"

"Denver." He wrinkled his nose.

"Oh! The interview. Yeah. Sure."

Weird. "Okay. We could leave Charlotte with Alice and Justin for a couple nights."

"That sounds great."

Liar.

He watched his daughter shove a piece of homemade ravioli into her mouth. "I have no idea what's going on around here, but I have job hunting to do." He left the kitchen in search of his laptop.

"Wait," Morgan yelled. "Not, yet. We, uh, wanted to play. Right, Charlotte?"

The little one bounced as she clapped. "Wets play! Wets play!"

Charlie crossed his arms and studied his girls. "What are you two up to?" Definitely something. Just like Alice.

Morgan shook her head. "Nothing."

He stalked her across the kitchen. "What do you think, Charly? Should I believe her, or should I tickle torture her until she tells me the truth?"

"Don't you dare!" Morgan held up her hands as she backed away from him.

Charlotte squealed.

Just as he reached for Morgan, the phone rang.

"Saved by the bell." He grinned as he picked up the cordless receiver. 'Private Number' registered on the Caller ID. "Hello?"

"Charlie, it's Will. Hey, uh, I know this is a strange request, but I've scheduled a private event at the bistro. Since you're still on the payroll, I didn't think you'd argue against cooking tomorrow night."

Tomorrow? Talk about short-ass notice. Charlie ran a hand across his head and looked at Morgan. Her eyes were wide with interest. Talk about not knowing how to answer. Charlie hadn't been sure he would ever cook in his bistro again. He still hadn't told the Mitchells he was officially leaving. Certainly, Alice had spilled the beans by now.

It might be a nice send-off to cook at the bistro a few more times. He could teach Corbin some things that would help the kid take charge. But tomorrow?

"I don't know, Will." He wandered down the hall as he talked. "Tomorrow may be too tight. There's a lot to do to get it ready to roll for a full service. I don't have a menu or fresh ingredients."

"Already taken care of. Supplies based off the last menu you prepared are being delivered to the bistro as we speak."

Charlie squeezed the back of his neck as he let that sink in. What the hell was going on around here? "A private party, huh?"

"Sort of a family thing," Will added.

That explained the rush and complete control Will had taken. Considering Charlie was about to leave the guy high and dry as soon as he found a job and another place to live, he supposed this was the least he could do. "Fine. What time should I be there?"

"Five o'clock should work. The servers will meet you there. All you'll have to do is cook."

When he returned to the kitchen, Morgan was cleaning Charlotte's face and hands at the sink.

"What was that about?" she asked.

"I'm going to cook for a private party at the bistro tomorrow night."

"Cool," she said, her gaze never lifting from their daughter's sticky fingers.

Maybe it was. He wasn't sure. Today had been so damn confusing. And he was absolutely convinced there was something shady going on here.

Chapter Seventeen

Charlie opened the alley door and stepped into the bistro for the first time in ten days. That number didn't seem too big, but the relief he felt when he stepped inside told him it'd been way too long.

He just missed cooking for a crowd. He'd get his fix tonight. Then he'd feel better. He wasn't going to get hung up on leaving this place.

"Hey, Chef." Corbin boxed him in the hallway, grinning from ear to ear. That goofy bow tie strangled his scrawny neck.

Charlie shook his head and smiled. "Hey, kid. Did you miss me?"

"I missed your red wine reduction sauce, ya know, since you won't tell me the secret ingredient so I can make it myself. But I did not miss your diva-like tirades."

Diva-like? For some reason, he pictured himself wearing rhinestones. It wasn't a good look. "I was kind of a jerk, wasn't I?

"Sometimes," Corbin said. "But I could handle it."

He shouldn't have had to. "I'm sorry. And to prove it I want you to stick around later tonight."

"For what?"

"So I can teach you the reduction." The lesson was long overdue. Besides, when he was gone from here, a part of him would remain in the bistro he'd built as long as someone was cooking his recipes.

Corbin tucked his chin to his chest and made a face. "Are you feeling okay?"

"Better than ever."

"I don't know if I can handle the power of a recipe like your red wine reduction. You sure?"

Charlie laughed. "Absolutely. Now, let's cut the mushy crap and get cooking. I want you on salads, desserts, and soups."

Corbin took two steps toward the kitchen, and then he stopped. "Wait a minute. You want me to cook … with you?"

"You're my sous chef. Of course you're cooking with me. The question is, if you're cooking, who's serving?"

"I am." Mark Mitchell stood at the serving counter dressed in a white button-down and black pants with an apron tied around his waist.

"And me." Justin stood beside him.

"And me." Will popped his head between them.

Charlie scrunched up his face. "Okay, I'm just going to say what I've been thinking for the last two days. What the fuck is going on?"

The Mitchell men laughed.

"You should probably ask the hostess," Corbin said.

Charlie could just imagine who the hostess was. Probably Margaret with a packed house of bridge club and bible study ladies bearing special requests up the old wazoo.

The closer he got to the dining room the more chatter he heard. Men's voices mixed with ladies' voice, and above it all was the squeal of a child. Charlotte? No. It couldn't be true. Why would she be here?

Charlie stopped and faced the men behind him again. "Whose party is this?"

"Once again, the hostess can give you the answers," Corbin said.

"Fuck you all." Charlie smiled. They were jerking his chain pretty good. "If I get out there and it's something bad, you better run."

But it wasn't bad. It was a dining room full of familiar, friendly faces, including Morgan, who stood at the hostess podium.

A quick glance around the room proved everyone was staring at him and wearing silly grins. Alice and Kory shared a corner table with Kory's parents, Ken and Carole. Jim Pierce, the grocer, and his wife, Susan, sat beside the Furhman Farm family. What an odd collection of people.

Again, a child squealed.

Charlie turned in time to see Aunt Phyllis hoisting his baby girl.

He narrowed his eyes on Morgan, whose smile looked shaky. Before he had a chance to say a word, someone tapped a glass.

The room quieted on an overpowering wave of shushes.

Morgan cleared her throat and glanced around the room. "I'd like to welcome everyone to Char-Grilled Bistro on a very special night. Chef Charlie Cramer … " she looked at him, "has been away from the kitchen for almost two weeks. As far as I'm concerned, that's way too long. And I intend to make sure that never happens again."

In the middle of a crowded room, all Charlie could hear was his breathing punctuated by the tapping of Morgan's shoes as she walked toward him.

"You are not leaving Harmony Falls, Charlie." She lifted his hands and laced her fingers with his. "You're staying in this town, in this restaurant, and in that house."

He opened his mouth to argue—he was going with her. But her next words ran right over his. "And I'm staying, too … with you … if you'll have me." She dropped to one knee. He could've heard a pin drop if his heartbeat wasn't echoing in his ears. "You're the only man I've every loved. You're the only man I ever will. Marry me?"

Whoops and whistles shattered the silence, as Charlie pulled her into his arms. All the times he thought something weird was going on … he never would've expected this.

Not in a million years.

"Yeah," he said into her ear. "I'll marry you anytime, anywhere. But, when we're alone tonight, you're going to have to explain exactly what happened here."

She laughed and he kissed her.

When they came up for air, he glanced around the room at the smiling faces. "So am I really cooking for all you people while the Mitchell brothers wait on you?"

More than one person shouted, "Hell, yeah!"

"Then let's get this show on the road."

And for the first time since Char-Grilled Bistro opened, the chef didn't complain about special orders and substitutions.

Especially when a little blonde girl asked for macaroni and cheese.

• • •

Three weeks after Morgan dropped to one knee inside the bistro, she donned a vintage wedding dress, pale pink lace and tulle, that Alice had stashed in the theater's costume closet. As she peeked out of Charlotte's bedroom blinds at the backyard tent streaming with ribbons and rose garlands Aunt Phyllis helped her make, Morgan felt overwhelmingly blessed.

Despite her mother's recent arrest.

Even when she'd heard the news, she hadn't felt like running away from who she was or what people might think of her. Why waste the effort? All the turmoil of the last three years led right back here anyway. It led her right back to where she was supposed to be.

She wasn't going to let anything chase her away from it again.

She sniffed.

"Do not cry and ruin that makeup." Alice's silver-gray pencil skirt and bolero jacket glistened in the sunlight streaming in from the window.

"I won't. I promise." Morgan dabbed beneath her eyes. "At least not until I officially say, 'I do.'"

Alice walked closer and smoothed the spaghetti strap on Morgan's right shoulder. "You look beautiful."

"Thank you."

She smoothed the other strap. "You know, I always wanted a sister. I just never in a gazillion years would've thought I wanted you."

The tears started up again, but Morgan kept them at bay with a roll of her eyes.

"You make my Charlie happy. That's all I've ever wanted in this whole wide world." She tilted her head. "Except for Justin. I'm really, really glad you wanted Charlie instead."

Morgan laughed. It was so damned warped it was funny.

They hugged as soft guitar music filtered in from the yard. It wouldn't be long, now. She'd be Mrs. Charlie Cramer before this day was through.

"Are we ready?" Aunt Phyllis passed Charlotte to Alice and walked to Morgan. With makeup and hair fixed to compliment her ivory wrap dress, Phyllis's transformation was shocking. She looked younger, happier, a bit like Morgan's mother used to look, except Aunt Phyllis had a heart so big it illuminated the room.

"You look amazing," Morgan said as she squeezed Aunt Phyllis's hands.

"You do, too." She leaned in and brushed the tip of her nose to Morgan's. "And there's a man out there in a tuxedo and cowboy boots who looks pretty darn good, too."

That man was waiting beneath an arbor just beyond the white reception tent. Charlie Cramer in a tuxedo. *Mm, mm, mm.* With one smile, he took her breath away.

Her promise not to cry was a big, fat joke.

Alice and Charlotte walked the grass runner to the final strains of "Somewhere over the Rainbow." Every so many steps, Charlotte tossed a handful of rose petals as if they were chicken feed. When a bird landed on a nearby folding chair, she attempted to bolt. But, Alice caught her, and lifted her into her arms amid laughter.

Those tears kept falling. With a smile, Morgan gave up trying to hold them in. She was entitled to every single one. This day was a long time coming.

The guitar music changed to "In My Life" by the Beatles, a song that resonated with her soul. Family and friends who had gathered around the arbor turned to face her. A lump of tears lodged in her throat.

"Here we go." Aunt Phyllis tightened her grip.

Sun blanketed the rich green grass, and a soft breeze ruffled the trees and fluttered Morgan's dress and hair. She walked slow and strong, trying to take it all in. She wanted to remember *this* wedding march.

There were smiles everywhere. Mark and Corbin. Mrs. Mitchell. Will and Kory. Hannah from the bistro, too. The small crowd brimmed with friendly faces. She never would've believed this was possible three months ago.

Her pace picked up when she looked at Charlie again. God, she loved him. As nice as it was to have all these other people here, he was all that mattered. Well, him and that little girl.

Charlotte waved as she bounced in Auntie Alice's arms. Justin was there, too, beside Charlie. Funny, he'd been waiting for her at the end of her last aisle walk, too.

She liked him much better in the role of best man.

Her gaze wandered back to Charlie. "I love you," she mouthed.

His smile could've outshone the sun. That man in a tuxedo, wearing cowboy boots, put every other man to shame.

She broke down again, blinking frantically, brushing tears off her cheeks when Charlotte reached for him, and he pulled her into his arms. They were going to be a family. A real family.

As the music faded, she took her place beneath the arbor. Aunt Phyllis grabbed Charlie's hand. For a moment, the people she loved most in the world were all connected. Then, Aunt Phyllis joined Morgan and Charlie's hands and with kisses to both their cheeks, backed away.

That was the last clear thing Morgan remembered. Time accelerated. The ceremony whizzed by with Charlotte in Charlie's arms, and her hand in his.

After they said their vows and shared a kiss, the justice of the peace announced, "Ladies and gentlemen, may I present to you, the Cramer family."

Even a fleeting thought about her parents couldn't wipe the smile off Morgan's face.

The Cramer family. She didn't think she'd ever heard more beautiful words.

As evening descended, white lights illuminated the reception tent and the delicious scent of Charlie's recipes, cooked by Corbin, wafted on the summer breeze.

They danced to acoustic guitar, laughed with guests, and when Charlotte finally crashed in Morgan's arms, snuck away as a family.

"I can't believe you're sneaking away from your own wedding reception," Charlie teased as they walked down the hall toward Charlotte's room. "What will people think of you?"

She grinned. "Me? What about you?"

"Oh, I'm not sneaking away. I'm just going to help my *wife* tuck in our little girl."

"Well then, I'm not sneaking away, either. I'm just going to put my little girl to bed—with help from my *husband*—and then I'm going to watch her sleep and count my blessings until her Aunt Phyllis comes in to lay with her. That poor woman is exhausted, too." Morgan chuckled. "What a day." A storybook day.

She eased Charlotte to the mattress and watched while Charlie pulled the covers over her. Blessing count: *two.* When Aunt Phyllis entered the room, Morgan counted *three*. Then, Charlie led her by the hand into the kitchen, where he brought her to face the window overlooking the back yard.

He wrapped his arms around her waist. "Look at that. Those are people celebrating our wedding day."

It sounded too good to be true. She lifted her lips to his jaw and kissed him. "Today was absolutely perfect. Like a dream come true."

He tightened his grip around her and nuzzled her neck. "My very favorite part was watching you walk down that aisle, knowing you were just steps away from being mine—forever."

She tipped her neck to one side, giving him better access, and reached behind her to thread fingers through his hair. "Yeah," she sighed. "That was very good."

"What was your very favorite part?" He dragged his lips across her neck.

"This part." She chuckled in between kisses. "Although, I do like having a last name I can be proud of. That feels really good. And the chocolate wedding cake. That was amazing as usual. The flower girl was exceptionally cute and well-behaved. God, there were so many very favorite parts."

"Pick *one*," he whispered in her ear.

"Fine. If I have to pick only one … it would be proving my parents wrong."

He turned her around and cupped her face. "About what?"

"About you." She smiled. "You weren't the wrong man for me, Charlie. You've been the right man all along." She lifted on her toes and brought her lips to within inches of his. "I'm so glad I finally decided to do something about it."

About the Author

Elley Arden is a born and bred Pennsylvanian who has lived as far west as Utah and as far north as Wisconsin. She drinks wine like it's water (a slight exaggeration), prefers a night at the ballpark to a night on the town, and believes almond English toffee is the key to happiness. Elley writes contemporary romances for Crimson Romance. For a complete list of Elley's books, visit www.elleyarden.com

More from This Author
(From *Battling the Best Man* by Elley Arden)

What was it about weddings that made perfectly sane people act like lunatics?

Kory pressed her bare back to the padded chair, adjusted the wide black belt strangling her ribcage just below her breasts, and fluffed the ruby red crinoline skirt, trying to get comfortable at the bridal table. She wouldn't be caught dead in this dress for any occasion other than her best friend's wedding. And now that the beautiful wedding part was over, Kory was subjected to this… people she'd known her whole life bumping and grinding all over the dance floor.

The principal? Kory cringed as she watched Russell Stonewall hike up the polyester fabric of his pants so he could squat lower as some song from an era long before her birth urged him to shake his booty. She looked away, scanning the crowd for a reasonable distraction only to find her mother wiggling her breasts and strutting around Kory's rhythmically challenged father. This was so not reasonable. Kory pushed fingers to her lips to halt the dry heave that arose.

The bride and groom danced on the outskirts of the chaotic circle. Alice floated on a pure white puff of crinoline as she sang the song word for word to Justin, one hand wrapped around his ruby red tie. He was laughing at the performance, and Kory found her lips twitching, too. God, those two were made for each other, and seeing them happy was worth any amount of discomfort Kory had to endure being back in her hometown.

"Your mother can groove." The deep voice added too many ooh's to groove as it slithered down the table, invading Kory's personal space.

She crossed her arms and tossed Will Mitchell a humorless look. She'd been trying to avoid him all weekend, but was failing miserably. They'd shared a rehearsal followed by a dinner, and a two-hour photo shoot followed by a cramped limousine ride. It was damn near impossible for the maid of honor to avoid the best man.

What were the odds her best friend would marry the brother of her high school nemesis? Kory had happily avoided Will for the past twelve years, which had been surprisingly easy since high school graduation what with her stifling training schedule and hundreds of miles between them. She'd only come home for the occasional holiday, having parents who preferred she stay in Chicago and conquer the medical world. Alice and Justin's whirlwind courtship hadn't left much time for socializing when Kory had been home, but she was certainly getting her fill of Will now.

"What's wrong, Doc? Too much education to appreciate a little dancing?"

No. Kory just had no desire to look like a fool shimmying in a disco ball-lit fish bowl. She didn't get the allure of participating in something she wasn't very good at. It seemed like wasted time. Not that sitting here, trying not to be dragged into meaningful conversation with the smuggest asshole she'd ever met was any more productive.

"I don't see you up there," she said.

"True."

Silence filtered between them along with a sense of satisfaction that she'd shut him up so quickly. He'd never been easy to beat. Back in high school, Will had managed every science fair win; every standardized test high score; and the pièce de résistance, valedictorian. Try as she might, she could never top him. She'd been a merit scholar and the most academically decorated female graduate in the history of Harmony Falls High School.

"What more could you want, honey?" her mother used to ask.

Juvenile or not, Kory had just wanted to beat him. She didn't want her accomplishments quantified by her gender. She didn't want to be the best female anything. She wanted to be the best. Period.

She blinked, and those scenes from the past dissipated. Her medical degree trumped his MBA, didn't it?

Maisy Carmichael wrapped a boa around Gilbert Hoover's neck and pressed her fuchsia-clad body against him. Gross didn't begin to describe it. Kory sighed and reached a sweaty hand to her head, digging at a bobby pin Maisy had cranked into place several hours ago. Painful—this whole damn thing was painful. Minus Alice being happy, of course. And that was what Kory had to remember, not that she was uncomfortable in this dress and ridiculous hairstyle, not that people in this town had no shame when it came to dancing, and not that she was sharing a table with the man who, after all these years, still managed to drive her nuts. It was like some bizarre switch got tripped when she was in his proximity, one that managed to warp her love for healthy competition into something crazed. Heck, she'd about clobbered the guy with her bouquet when he'd managed to win that dumb bridal party scavenger hunt in the limo on the way here. It had been awfully suspicious that he just happened to have a penny in his pocket from the year the bride was born. Was he really that good or was he just that lucky?

He was a Mitchell, after all.

Kory glanced down the table, where he lounged seemingly in mid-execution of a formidable Ben Affleck impression—aloof but oddly attractive. It annoyed the crap out of her. His chair sat too far from the table, and he reclined in it, legs long and slanted, left arm slung along the back of the chair beside him. He was slouching, literally slouching, and that struck her as particularly annoying since he was a thirty-year-old dressed in a tuxedo. *Sit the hell up*, she wanted to say, but she bit her bottom lip instead and turned her gaze back to the dance floor.

Four beats of the music later, he was sliding into the chair beside her.

"How's Chicago?"

"Windy," she answered, her tone clipped. What she really wanted to say was, "Amazing, teeming with vibrant life and opportunity—things you don't have here." Because after all the time and effort the Mitchell family had put into saving this town from economic decay and population decline, the reminder they still had so far to go was bound to irk him. Irking him would feel good. But saying all that meant saying more to him than she wanted to, so she kept it short, but hardly sweet.

"You're doing some medical training thing, right? Alice mentioned it. How's that going?"

Medical training thing? Somehow Kory managed not to roll her eyes. "It's a traumatic brain injury fellowship, and it's challenging." In the best way possible. The move away from Harmony Falls to a major city had afforded Kory challenges and experiences she never would've found in this closed-minded little town, where the mailman had once informed her that men were doctors and women were nurses. As furious as that had made her, she considered the source. These people bought chewing tobacco in bulk and thought the first day of buck was worthy of a holiday. In one short month she'd be graduated from fellowship and ready to take her place as assistant medical director of the in-patient rehabilitation unit at the world-renowned Chicago Northern Rehab Institute. She'd have a prestigious title, a fat salary, and too many cultural experiences to count.

Beat that, Will Mitchell.

"So…uh…how much calculus do you use on a daily basis?"

She looked at him through squinted eyes, a pinch in her chest telling her exactly where this was going. "Excuse me?"

"You know, calculus? We were in that class together in high school." His grin turned wolfish as he gave her a very obvious once over. "Let me tell you. If you'd looked like this back then, I never would've passed."

Kory glared at him. Did he seriously not remember what had happened in that class? They'd *both* tested out of the usual Algebra classes offered to ninth-graders at Harmony Falls High—the only two in their class to do so. In Calculus, he'd been like a ten-year-old, poking his pencil between her shoulder blades, tugging on her ponytail, and cracking gum in her ear—but Kory hadn't minded. Will had been one of the cutest boys in the class and his playful teasing had made her feel special, like they were friends, facing a senior-level math class together. She'd found the attention from an attractive, smart, and charismatic guy charming.

Not charming, however, was the way it escalated. Unlike Kory who didn't even like to raise her hand in class, gregarious, funny Will had been able to fit in quickly and easily with the senior boys. After a few weeks, his new friends started teasing her too, but without the playfulness Will had. Instead, they cracked overtly sexual jokes that made her crazily uncomfortable. *Kory, what do math and my dick have in common? They're both hard for you.* That one had brought her to tears. Anger at their taunts and disappointment that Will—whom she'd thought was her friend— hadn't stood up for her but had laughed along with them made her even more withdrawn. The teacher and principal got involved and punished the boys, but it had been as if Kory was punished, too. Despite her ability to handle the classwork and her protests, the principal had also transferred her back to Honors Algebra. Will had remained in calculus, the only freshman in a senior-level class. And she hated him for it.

Once, when Will was without his entourage, he'd stopped her in the hallway between classes, and she'd suspected he was going to apologize, but she'd walked away before he could say a word—she'd felt too betrayed to accept an olive branch. He'd barely spoken to her after that, which was probably best. By then, Kory didn't trust him, and she had vowed revenge, working extra hard to beat his scores.

Thankfully, things were different now. Dr. Kory Flemming was successful in a male-dominated field, which meant she hadn't so much as blushed in years. Whatever Will had hoped to accomplish by bringing up the calculus topic tonight wasn't going to happen.

With a shove, she pushed away from the table and stood. "Calculus," she said with a bitchy grin. "I remember it well. I learned a valuable lesson in that class."

"What's that?" he asked, smiling up at her.

"That you're a dick." She spun around on the bare balls of her feet and charged the dance floor.

• • •

Will watched her go, the smile fading from his face. First words she'd said to him all damn weekend and she'd insulted him. Then again, he probably deserved it. His booze-soaked brain had been scrambling, trying to come up with something, *anything* that might get more than a one-word answer from Kory. He'd succeeded, but at what cost? After that hostile exchange, he wasn't likely to get another word out of her for the rest of the night. What a shame.

They'd been friends when they were little. Teachers were always sticking them together for some project or another. But by high school, they'd gone their separate ways. The truth was Calculus was the only class he could think of that they'd had together. And apparently it was a sore point. That or Kory didn't take kindly to his attempt at flattery. Although she was definitely better looking now than she had been in high school, he probably should've tried a subtler compliment.

Shit. He thought about going after her, because Alice would read him the riot act if she thought he was being mean to her best friend, but he didn't trust his liquored-up self not to say something even worse, maybe something about tangent curves. After all these years, he didn't know her very well, but from the way she reacted to his previous come on, he wouldn't be surprised if a similar comment came with a slap across his face. Besides, watching her now, he couldn't see many curves. From the top of her bronze head to the tip of her honey-colored toes, she was long and lean, straight and strong.

She grabbed her mother's hand and then her father's and the trio did some awkward square dance move, shrinking the circle and then widening it again to the rhythm of a popular rap song. Will hoped she was a better doctor than she was a dancer, a thought that had him chuckling against the rim of his whiskey glass. He knew she didn't want to be out there, but the alternative was being here with him, and apparently that was a worse kind of torture—because he was a dick. Flinching, he swallowed another hefty mouthful of liquor.

The alcohol burned a path from his throat to his stomach, and he sucked cake-scented air into his nose. He caught sight of his smiling brother, and managed to smile, too. He was happy for Justin and Alice. He really was. But he would've been even happier had they eloped.

Justin approached from the opposite side of the table, and reached for his water glass. "You mean to tell me out of all these beautiful women you can't find one to dance with?"

Will looked at Kory, which was a laughable direction for his attentions to take. After their exchange, she'd be the last beautiful woman in this room to dance with him. Hell, she'd already managed to weasel her way out of their one official dance by partnering with the ring bearer and insisting Will dance with the flower girl.

He glanced at his brother. "If I'm dancing, I can only appreciate one of them at a time. From this vantage point, it's equal opportunity admiration."

"You're full of it." Justin skirted the table, and sat. "One of these days you're going to realize there's more to life than hefty profit margins at work and an Australian Shepard in your bed."

"Never." Will opened his mouth for an extra-large swig of whiskey.

Justin's hand landed hard on Will's shoulder. "I used to think success was measured by bankrolls and titles, too, but look at her."

The *her* Justin referred to was Alice no doubt, and Will obliged, scanning the dance floor until he found his smiling sister-in-law.

"She glows," Justin said. "She literally lights up my life. Before her, there was only darkness."

Will looked at the water glass in Justin's hand. "Please tell me you've had more than that to drink, because if you're saying all that sober, after Morgan Parrish cheated on you and made your last attempt at a wedding a laughing stock, while—may I remind you—simultaneously destroying your congressional career," Will said, shooting an incredulous glare at his brother, "I might just have to smack you."

Justin whistled. "First of all, that's ancient history, and second, damn, it's no wonder you're sitting alone. You're a real downer. You need to work on that, bro. This is a wedding."

"Yeah, a wedding. It's a fairytale for one night. But it isn't real." His gaze automatically skipped to his widowed mother who sat alone at a nearby table. "Reality is the so-called lucky ones finding somebody tolerable, getting married, and annoying the shit out of each other for decades, until one of them finally dies, leaving the other one an emotional void."

Dad had been dead for decades, but Will remembered what their mother had been like before cancer obliterated the man. He had a singular, sharp memory of her sitting at their long dining table with Aunt Dorothy, laughing until she cried, her whole body shaking at some joke. He'd never heard her laugh like that again. It was like she'd shut off everything the day Dad died—the laughter, the warmth, the love. All she lived for now was the family business. Will tucked a finger into his shirt collar and pulled, making some room for the next swallow of whiskey.

Justin stared at him for a long moment, and then shook his head. He drained his water glass and stood. "Before I return to my glowing bride, who is infinitely better company than you, let me remind you that even when our father was alive, our mother was never a naturally happy woman, and despite all the bad things that happened to me, I'm here, happier than I ever dreamed I could be." He squeezed Will's shoulders. "I'd rather be mayor of Harmony Falls with Alice by my side than President of the United States with Morgan Parrish any day. Sometimes when you lose you win." After one more squeeze, he walked away.

Will sat there, polishing off the whiskey. His gaze wandered back to Kory who seemed to be using her parents as a shield, but not shield enough for him to lose sight of her completely. Her long arms remained locked at the elbows, and her bare shoulders were tight and square. He pushed fingers against his throat and rubbed at some sort of discomfort as she tossed her head side to side, the blunt ends of her straight hair whipping her jawline.

She looked at him, an icy glare that changed before she looked away. It didn't soften, but it definitely lost some of its intensity. And when she looked at him again—fast enough for him to miss it if he blinked—it was something else entirely. Pricks of pleasure scattered across the back of his neck and crawled onto his face. And they were perplexing as hell, because she hated him. Didn't she? She'd barely talked to him all weekend.

Let's think about this for a minute... But the liquor melted more than everything in its path, turning his belly into a bucket of jelly and his brain into a dehydrated sponge. He reached for an unattended plate of wedding cake and polished it off.

"I totally take offense to people not dancing at my wedding." Alice seemed to come out of nowhere, plopping down in Kory's chair and grabbing the long-stem glass of champagne Kory had neglected.

"Did my brother tell you to come over here and *glow* on me so I'd quit being a wallflower and find a suitable dance partner?"

"He may have mentioned you being moody." She drank, leaving a vivid lipstick print on the rim. "I also saw you talking to Kory, which didn't seem to end well. Were you picking on her again?"

"More like reminiscing," Will lied, dropping the fork and rubbing a palm against the back of his overheated neck. He told himself not to, but he lifted his gaze to the lady in question. She was still dancing, if that was what one could call it. It was more like jerking with a little thrusting thrown in, and...*damn*. He closed his eyes and shook his head.

"You know, if you keep picking on her, she's going to think you like her."

His nose twitched as he looked at his new sister-in-law. "We're not in elementary school, Alice."

"Exactly. So grow up, Will. Stop looking like you want to pass her a note that involves checking yes or no." She swatted his arm and threw back her head for a cackle. "Or is that how you ask all your dates out? Because it might explain why you never seem to have any..." She batted pitch-black eyelashes and pursed her lips.

He did not want to talk about his lack of a meaningful social life or the fact that he felt more comfortable with things he could measure and compute. Who wanted to spend life tethered to something abstract like what another person thought and felt? It was too subjective for him—too ripe for real rejection. Fortunately, as a wealthy, decent-looking, single man, he didn't have to risk much to find a willing woman for his bed. The hard part was dealing with her disappointment when she realized he wasn't going to change his mind about having anything close to a relationship. That sort of thing just wasn't for him.

"I'm perfectly happy being single, Alice. I can work as many hours as I like, close as many deals as I can, and I don't have to worry about sharing the profits with anybody."

"Sounds lonely," Alice said, adding a pout.

If Will were being honest, he'd admit sometimes it was, but lonely was a hell of a lot easier than finding someone whose eyes didn't glaze over when he started talking about the law of diminishing marginal returns. That sort of reaction was no ego boost, and it was exhausting trying to hide part of him simply so he could keep somebody by his side. It was better to keep things casual. That way nobody got to know what was buried beneath the Mitchell polish.

"Come on." Alice stood and grabbed his hands. "Let's dance." She tugged, jumping to the disco beat.

Will stayed put. "Don't you have some theatre donor to schmooze?"

"At my wedding reception? That would be tacky. Besides, Justin is busy gathering support for his mayoral run."

Because *that* wasn't tacky. Will managed to keep his eyes from rolling while Alice ducked beneath one of his raised arms and twirled. She danced around him like he was reciprocating, and he suddenly felt like the miserable fool Justin had accused him of being. This was a wedding. His big brother was right; Will needed to work on his mood. He stood, smiling at Alice's shocked squeal when he spun her around again.

"There you go!" She pulled him away from the table. "Three more steps and you'll be on the dance floor."

He'd had just enough whiskey to make following her seem reasonable.

"I'm in shock." Justin said when they'd reached the dance floor.

Alice released one of Will's hands and laced her fingers with her husband's. "He's not as boring as you think he is."

Maybe not boring, but he sure felt like a third wheel. Will released Alice's other hand but not before he gave it a squeeze. "Thank you."

"You're welcome." She kissed him on the cheek. "But you're not allowed to sit down again. Got it?"

Will nodded. "I'm just going to find my own partner."

"Excellent. Our job here is done," Justin said, spinning his bride toward the center of the floor. "We'll be watching you."

Will shook his head and smiled at the goofy, wide-eyed look his brother gave, and then he set his sights on the crowd. There had to be someone who would tolerate his mediocre dance moves and not mistake his offer to dance for something more.

His mother still sat alone, surprisingly without his younger brother Mark, who was better known as her shadow. Asking her was probably the least complicated option.

"Mother," Will said, inclining his head when he reached her side. "May I have this dance?"

She wrinkled her narrow nose as she watched the dance floor. "I've danced enough for one night."

Will winced at the easy brush-off. He'd seen her dance exactly twice: once with Mark during the bridal party dance, and once with Justin during the mother-son dance. He didn't want to take it personally, so he told himself even two years after her heart attack, she hadn't regained all of her strength, but it was hard not to feel rejected. With hands in his pockets, he glanced at the full dance floor, having lost his drive to change his mood. Maybe he'd just sit here and talk business. At least his position and achievements as Chief Operating Officer of Mitchell Company, Inc. could be counted on to endear him to his CEO mother.

"I sent Mark for drinks," she continued, and then she looked at him. "Well, don't just stand there blocking my view. Either sit or move along."

On second thought, there had to be a better option for company.

"Enjoy your drinks," he said, deciding he'd rather deal with Justin and Alice's disappointment over seeing him back in his seat at an empty table than weather his mother's sour attitude and disapproval.

He'd only made it halfway across the dance floor, when Carole Flemming caught his eye.

"Will," she preened, sweeping toward him, dragging Kory behind her. "This is beautiful! Your family sure knows how to put on a wedding."

Money could do that for a person, money and Alice Cramer Mitchell's flair for the dramatic. He took a quick glance at the glistening red and gold ballroom and smiled. "Thank you. You look like you're having a good time."

"Oh, I am."

Kory was dead silent. She'd moved on from holding hands with her mother to locking elbows with the woman. And she was looking everywhere but at him.

"But I'm beat," Mrs. Flemming added. "Kory is suddenly an Energizer bunny."

On that comment, Kory's emerald eyes widened to full moon proportion. "Well, I…"

"Should dance with Will," Mrs. Flemming said, shoving her daughter toward him. "He doesn't have a partner. Do you, Will?"

Will shook his head. "I do not, and my brother and his new wife made it perfectly clear I need to find one."

Kory stepped back. "On second thought, I *am* tired."

"Nonsense." Mrs. Flemming smacked her daughter's hand a few times and pulled away from her grip. "Dance for heaven's sake. Once you get back to Chicago it will be all work and no play."

If Kory's teeth were nails, Will had no doubt she would've spit a mouthful at him.

"Come on, Kory. It's one dance. Don't tell me you're afraid I'll be so good I'll make you look bad."

"Hardly." She huffed but took a step closer. "One dance, Will, and only because I don't want to disappoint my mother, but I'm warning you. If you mention calculus, I'll knee you in the balls and walk away."

He chuckled. "Deal." Sliding a hand around her waist and pulling her closer, his laughter evaporated. For a skinny woman, she sure was soft, which may have had something to do with the miles of satin covering her. He opened his mouth for a shallow breath, drawing her the last couple inches against his chest, getting a mouthful of air tinged with something even sweeter than wedding cake. His rusty libido groaned. Somewhere in the distance beyond the physical sensations of Kory's palm pressing against the back of his neck…and her fingernails grazing his hairline…and her opposite hand nestled hot and tight in his…his brain whispered to his body, *she's not interested in you.*

Acoustic guitar music registered, and then her breath tickled his earlobe. He froze for a moment before instinct had him twisting his wrist and rotating her arm so he could hold her hand against his chest. Swallowing was inexplicably difficult, so he cleared his throat to aid the process, and felt her body tense.

He should've stayed at the table with his mother. At least he knew where he stood over there. Here, he was just a man, feeling things for a woman, who, he was damn near certain, wasn't feeling anything at all for him.

"You know, you can speak? When I said don't mention calculus, I wasn't suggesting we dance in awkward silence."

He nodded, loosened his fingers around her hand, and lightened his palm on her back. "I'm sorry. I'm trying to behave. It seems like I say something stupid every time I open my mouth around you."

Tipping her head back, Kory studied him. Her brows pulled together, wrinkling her forehead, and her glossy lips pursed. She looked…beautiful. Will squeezed his eyes shut for a split second, trying to reset his brain.

"That's the smartest thing you've said all weekend." She released a bona fide chuckle that lit her green eyes and showed off the prettiest smile.

Will laughed, too, and that bit of cordial commiseration fanned the spark in his gut. *Bad idea*, his brain said. *She still doesn't like you.* But his body had a mind of its own, pulling her closer until she settled her chin on his shoulder and somewhat relaxed.

Apparently, sixteen years hadn't changed a thing. When Kory Flemming was near, Will Mitchell acted like a fool.

He noted the song winding down and battled a burst of disappointment, because he wasn't ready for her to leave—not when they were finally playing nicely. A few strands of silky hair brushed his lips, and he darted out his tongue, taking a not-so-innocent taste. He really was a strange bird.

"You know, when I get back to Chicago tomorrow night, I'm going straight to ophthalmology and requesting they zap my eyes with laser. Maybe they can erase some of the whacked out things I've seen since I've been back here." This was more than she'd said to him the entire weekend, and all he could take away from it was she was leaving tomorrow. He had no idea when she'd be back again, especially with her poor opinion of small-town Harmony Falls. And that felt like a terrible shame.

Suddenly, he wanted to alter their entire history or at least press rewind on the weekend. Maybe with more time he could've found his footing with her, and they could've had a little fun. After all, she was the only person he knew who might share his excitement over the discovery of a Higgs boson subatomic spec. Then again, if her mother was right, fun—scientific or otherwise—didn't seem to be a high priority to Dr. Flemming.

"Is it true what your mother said?" Will asked.

"What did my mother say?"

"That Chicago is all work and no play?"

"I like to work."

He could appreciate that. Heck, he lived that way, too. "You don't like to play?"

A charged silence lingered between them, and the music changed to a fast song not conducive to holding her close, but she surprised him by not backing away.

"I play," she whispered.

A hot flush greater than anything the whiskey had delivered heated Will from the inside out.

"Get a room," Mark called as he cut across the crowded dance floor, two highball drinks in hand.

That did the trick. Kory rocketed from Will's arms like he'd burst into flames—he felt like he did. She blinked fast and furious, adjusting the belt around her waist. "Thanks for the dance," she managed before scurrying away.

Will turned to his younger brother and glared. "Nice."

Mark laughed. "Here." He held out a small glass of amber liquor. "Consolation."

Will threw it back, because, hell, he'd rather be drunk and numb than wondering why he was hot for Kory Flemming after all these years.

For more books by Elley Arden, check out:

Crashing the Congressman's Wedding

Save My Soul

Change My Mind

Heal My Heart

Baby By Design

Chad's Chance in the Emerald Springs Legacy series

And look for her Kemmon Brothers novella in *Take Me Out*

In the mood for more Crimson Romance?
Check out *Daniel's Decision* in the *Emerald Springs Legacy* series
by Nicole Flockton at *CrimsonRomance.com*.

www.ingramcontent.com/pod-product-compliance
Lightning Source LLC
Chambersburg PA
CBHW010309100726
47905CB00011B/3274